"I swear I don't know a thing . . . !"

Quark quickly assured Captain Benjamin Sisko as their eyes met.

"Well, somebody must," Sisko said.

"Oh, come on, Captain," Quark said. "With all the ships in this region of space, you can't seriously expect me to know every little—"

"Captain," Worf interrupted. "The intruder is now targeting the ship you are on."

"All right, Quark," Sisko said sternly, stepping closer to the Ferengi, bending slightly, leaving only a few centimeters of space between the two of them. He pointed toward the ship beyond the view port. "I am running out of patience. For the last time, who are they, and what do they want?"

STAR TREK
DEEP SPACE NINE®

TRIAL BY ERROR

Mark Garland

POCKET BOOKS

New York   London   Toronto   Sydney   Tokyo   Singapore

An *Original* Publication of POCKET BOOKS

POCKET BOOKS, a division of Simon & Schuster Inc.
1230 Avenue of the Americas, New York, NY 10020

This book is published by Pocket Books, a division of
Simon & Schuster Inc., under exclusive license from
Paramount Pictures.

ISBN: 0-671-00251-1

First Pocket Books printing November 1997

10 9 8 7 6 5 4 3 2 1

POCKET and colophon are registered trademarks of
Simon & Schuster Inc.

Printed in the U.S.A.

TRIAL BY ERROR

CHAPTER
1

"ON-SCREEN!" CAPTAIN DOLRAS snapped, lowering himself into the command chair. He leaned forward and stared at the main viewscreen. What was that strange dark cloud?

The other Klingons around him fell silent. None of the gruff banter that normally broke the monotony of space travel now, Dolras thought, allowing himself a mental nod. Yes, they were a good crew, even if they had to serve aboard a military freighter like the *Toknor.*

Now, with only the electronic chatter of instrument consoles and the soft, habitual ratcheting sound of the crew's leather vestments breaking the silence, Dolras looked to his left, to Lieutenant Kotren. His science officer might be young, but Dolras expected nothing less than excellence from him, and he expected it now. "Sensor update!"

Kotren stared at his screens, a puzzled look on his face. He didn't know what was out there either, Dolras realized. None of them had ever seen anything like it.

"We still lack positive readings," Kotren said. "I am recalibrating the primary array."

Disgruntled, Dolras turned his attention back to the main viewscreen. The forward image showed only a vague, hazy, clouded area of space with no clear boundaries. Yet it showed up as an energy field of some kind.

"The anomaly continues to block our path," said Thrann, Dolras's first officer, who had taken the helm at his captain's request.

Dolras squinted as he leaned forward, baring his sharp teeth, privately savoring his own instinctive reaction, that of a hunter considering his prey, a warrior sizing up a possible foe. Space travel had changed the Klingon heart very little, had not lessened the unfailing urge to embrace confrontation, to accept challenge, Dolras thought. But he needed more than instinct here. Passion alone would not make the image or a proper course of action any clearer.

His mission was a simple one: survey a sector of what the High Council considered non-Dominion space in the Gamma Quadrant, collect sensor data and geological samples, and then return to the Alpha Quadrant. The risk lay in determining if the sector truly *was* outside the Dominion's primary boundaries—which, as far as Dolras was concerned, had proven to be the case.

Several unknown vessels had dogged his trail from time to time, but none had dared to challenge him. In fact, except for the odd cloud, the mission had been quite unremarkable. There had, however, been one other exception.

Two days ago the *Toknor* had encountered the remains of a Karama ship—the Karama were a race known to do business with the Jem'Hadar. The ship had been almost completely destroyed, and there was ample evidence to attribute its destruction to extremely high-energy weapons fire. Since establishing their recent presence in Cardassian space, officers of the Klingon Empire had gathered a considerable amount of intelligence on the Jem'Hadar. While it was true that the Jem'Hadar possessed formidable weapons, the *Toknor*'s computer could not attribute the Karama ship's destruction to any of them.

Two unknowns, Dolras thought, still observing the second one. He didn't like it. Could there be a connection?

Dolras had stayed near the Karama ship as long as he could, examining unremarkable long-range sensor reports. Then he had moved on, deeper into the Gamma Quadrant and farther away from Dominion space, all the while wondering what was out there waiting for them.

So far he considered the mission a success because it had resulted in a considerable store of new planetary and even some cultural data of the kind that could be analyzed to provide valuable trade and military intelligence. And Klingon mission parameters did not necessarily include the investigation of space phenomena, which ordinarily was all well and good to Dolras's mind. But this unidentified energy field had been following his freighter ever since the *Toknor* had left orbit around a small, rather unremarkable planetoid roughly one-quarter light-year back. Sometimes it was ahead of them, and sometimes it was behind. It almost seemed to be studying them.

At present the energy cloud lay dead ahead. But not for long, if Dolras had anything to say about it.

"Evasive maneuvers, Thrann," Dolras told his first officer. "Maximum impulse." He would see exactly what their little cloud did.

Thrann quickly complied.

Dolras watched as the ghostly patch of space, some five hundred meters across, appeared to remain stationary in the viewer as the *Toknor* changed course.

"The field continues to pace us," Thrann reported.

Dolras frowned. "How far are we from the wormhole?" They were in no immediate jeopardy, as far as he could tell, but this anomaly was becoming a real concern.

4

"At warp six, two-point-one days," Thrann said.

That was nearly the maximum sustainable speed for the *Toknor,* but Dolras knew he could squeeze warp six-five out of her for at least two-point-one days. And in any case, there was no reason to believe the anomaly was capable of warp speeds. The *Toknor* had been completing a sensor sweep, traveling at three-quarters impulse since leaving the vicinity of the planetoid.

"Bring us one hundred eighty degrees about," Dolras ordered. He watched closely as the anomaly circled to the *Toknor*'s stern. Good, he thought.

"Set a direct course for the wormhole and prepare to go to warp. But wait for my order." Dolras looked up. "Kotren!"

"Sir?"

"Tell us something worthwhile!"

His science officer turned, forehead ridges damp with sweat, his expression intensely serious.

"I am still evaluating our data," Kotren said.

Our lack of data, Dolras thought. He knew Kotren was giving his captain and crew everything he had. Some years ago, Dolras would have censured the young officer even so, but not now. *Not yet,* he told himself. He had been in space for too many decades; he preferred to save his energies for times that truly required them. Whatever phenomena his ship had encountered, it was clearly outside even the computer's knowledge.

Dolras steadied himself. "This thing is playing a

game with us. I want to know more about it. Prepare a sensor probe for launch. We will investigate this energy field up close and find out why it insists on following us."

"At once!" Kotren said.

"The probe data may make it possible for you to determine the cloud's purpose," Dolras continued. *If it has one,* he thought. But he suspected it did, and he was intent on determining what that purpose was.

"The probe is ready," Kotren announced a moment later.

Dolras looked to the main viewer. "Launch!"

"Probe launched," Kotren said.

"On screen," Dolras said. The low-pitched *ping* of the departing probe resounded through the ship, and he watched the main viewer as the tiny machine propelled itself across the narrow gulf between the *Toknor* and its unwelcome shadow.

"We're receiving specific telemetry and sensor data," Kotren began.

Dolras watched the probe vanish into the energy field, almost as if it had been absorbed.

"The field is chiefly composed of positively charged plasma particles," Kotren continued. Then he fell silent.

"Continue!" Dolras demanded. He had to know what was happening.

"Sir, we have lost contact with the probe," Kotren said. "I am attempting to reestablish—"

"Then what is that?" Dolras snapped, leaping to

his feet. He jabbed his finger at the screen as the probe—the same probe they had just launched—exited the thin, cloudy anomaly and arced back toward the *Toknor*. He took a step toward the screen.

"I see it, Captain," Kotren replied, glancing frantically from the screen to his consoles and back. "But we are receiving no telemetry. The probe no longer registers on our sensors."

Dolras narrowed his eyes. It did not register? How could that be? He could *see* it. "Turn it around and send it back," he said evenly, sitting again.

Kotren attempted to comply, then turned back to his captain. "We still have no control over the probe."

"Thrann!" Dolras shouted. "Regain control of the probe. If that is not possible, put a tractor beam on it!"

Dolras watched Thrann tap at his controls, then shake his head. He worked again, and Dolras watched the screen as the pale orange light of the ship's tractor beam reached out and engulfed the probe . . . and the probe passed through it.

"I cannot explain it," Thrann said, his voice tense. "The beam is having no effect. It is as if there is no probe there to lock on to."

"Then destroy the probe," Dolras said. He nodded to himself. That would certainly solve the problem. "Target disrupters."

"Powering disrupters. Target acquired," Thrann said.

"Fire!"

Dolras saw the beam strike out at the probe—and pass straight through it with no apparent affect.

As he noted the probe's course, Dolras needed no instruments to tell him what would happen next. "Shields up," he ordered. "Prepare for impact!"

He braced himself as the probe arrived at the *Toknor,* but instead of the expected impact and explosion, the probe passed through the shields with only a flicker of color, then continued into the ship itself. No contact was felt.

"Report!"

"No impact registered," Thrann said. "The probe seems to have vanished."

Dolras swore under his breath as he stared once more at the anomaly—this strange curiosity that was well on its way to becoming his most vexing adversary. Still, the cloud seemed to present no immediate danger of any kind, only an unsettling mystery to be solved. He frowned. He didn't like mysteries.

"Close to within two hundred thousand kilometers," he told Thrann. "Modify our forward disrupter array to emit a diffused electrostatic charge, reverse polarity."

"That could disrupt the cloud's entire energy field," Kotren said.

"Or it could send that thing, whatever it is, running for home. Either way there will be sparks enough to see what it looks like with a light shining on it."

Thrann acknowledged Dolras's comment and went about the task. A moment later he raised his head. "Ready," he said.

"Watch it closely, Lieutenant," Dolras told Kotren. "This is our only chance to learn something. Thrann, are we ready to go to warp?"

"Yes, Captain."

"Activate the disruptor array."

Dolras leaned back, watching the main viewer, as a bright red beam of electrostatic energy hit the cloud. It began to seethe with movement. Yellows, oranges, and pinks swirled this way and that. Dolras gaped. It was beautiful, almost mesmerizing.

Seconds later a blinding light burst from the cloud. Dolras shielded his eyes while the computer compensated for the increased brightness.

"What was that?" he demanded of Kotren. "Status!"

Warning klaxons abruptly sounded. Dolras tried to blink the white-hot spots from his eyes, to no avail.

"We are being bombarded with an intense wide-spectrum radiation beam," Kotren replied. "Every system on the ship is approaching overload status. Recommend—"

"Go to warp, Thrann!" Dolras shouted. "Engage, engage!"

"Coming about," Thrann reported, hastily manipulating the helm controls. "Engaging now."

On the screen, the stars spun in a quarter circle, then sprang back to became long, narrow lines of light that seemed to stream away in all directions. Dolras took a deep, calming breath. Perhaps the disruptor array had been a mistake. But at least they were safe now.

"Captain," Thrann said after a moment, "the energy field is pursuing us, matching speed and course, continuing to accelerate."

Dolras felt a hardness in his stomach. Warp speeds, it seemed, were not an advantage.

"I have it on aft visual," Kotren said. "The field seems to be changing, taking on a distinct shape."

"Put it on the main screen," Dolras told him. "Maximum magnification."

To his surprise the image that sprang into view was nothing like the cloud. It had come together into a vague blocky shape, and though it was indistinct, he recognized the lines of a long hull and warp engines.

"A starship," Thrann said.

"So it would appear," Dolras said. But who were they? What did they want? "Identification?"

"None yet," Thrann said. "Our sensors cannot pick it up."

"Impossible," Dolras scoffed, clenching one fist as the frustration built within him. "I have never heard of a cloaking device like this, but now that it is down, we should be getting *some* readings."

"Their technology must be well beyond our own," Thrann said grimly. "I recommend firing on it, with or without a lock."

"First, open hailing frequencies," Dolras said. "Tell them to identify themselves and break off their pursuit, or we will open fire. Thrann, prepare a photon torpedo."

Both officers did as they were told.

"No response to our hails," Kotren said a minute later.

"Torpedo ready," Thrann said.

Dolras closed one eye and fixed the other on the dark object still following his freighter. He felt a twinge of earned pleasure. Enough was enough. "Fire torpedo," he said.

"Torpedo fired."

"Tactical onscreen," Dolras said, and the desired display filled the main viewer. He watched the computer's representation of the torpedo as it traversed the distance between ships. It appeared to strike the target precisely.

"Direct hit," Thrann reported. "No detonation. No effect."

"How is that possible?" Dolras said, coming halfway out of his seat, then lowing himself heavily back down. He clutched the arms of his command chair.

"The torpedo has vanished," Thrann replied.

"Fire again! Fire at will!"

Dolras watched a second torpedo track toward its target as precisely as the first, followed by yet another. Both quickly vanished, leaving their objective untouched.

"Torpedo detected on course toward us," Thrann

announced, and Dolras heard the agitation in his voice. Despite their training and seasoning, his crew members had little actual combat experience. Still, they were Klingons: they would perform their duties, and he would do the same.

"Divert as much power as possible to aft shields," he said. "Target incoming torpedo."

"Enemy torpedo closing," Kotren announced. "Configuration unknown. I am reading it as a high energy plasma burst."

"Fire!" Dolras ordered. If they could detonate the enemy torpedo before it hit their ship, they would be spared the worst of its effects.

Thrann fired the *Toknor*'s fourth torpedo. Dolras tensed as it flew a brief intercept course and met the incoming torpedo exactly.

"No effect," Thrann said.

Dolras sat back. No such thing was possible, and yet . . .

"Brace for impact," he said.

As the words left the captain's mouth, the *Toknor* heaved suddenly forward, then shook with a violence even he was not prepared for. The aft screen went instantly white with brightness from the explosion. Around him, power relays overloaded. The bridge went dark, lit only by flashes and sparks from instrument panels as numerous systems shorted out.

Dolras held on to his chair, teeth bared, growling deep in his throat, finding no words to express his fury. Smoke filled his nose and throat. He watched his Ops officer scramble to put out a fire that had started near the science station. Blood and burn-marks streaked the side of his face.

Dolras forced his growl to become a speaking voice. "Status!"

"The impact of the plasma burst nearly collapsed the aft shields," Thrann reported. "I am attempting to compensate."

Dolras rose and made his way across the bridge to Thrann's station. The *Toknor* was already at warp six-point-three, the fastest speed anyone could expect from such a ship. He watched the readout change: warp six-point-four. His mission was to return with the information and samples he had spent so many months gathering—not a glorious mission, perhaps, but an important one nonetheless. He did not intend to fail.

"Continue on course for the wormhole," Dolras said. He tapped at the console's intercom control.

"Engineering, I want everything you can give me, do you hear? Warp seven would be a good start!"

"Yes, sir!" came his chief engineer's resounding reply.

Good, Dolras thought. Someone knew how to respond to an emergency.

"When we reach the Alpha Quadrant, we can arrange to rendezvous with a Klingon attack force," Dolras told Thrann privately. "Together we will know victory, and we will finally learn who is behind this."

Thrann nodded.

Dolras reached out and tapped the main controls,

removing the tactical display from the main screen and restoring the external forward view. Then he stood back, staring at the image in silence.

"Captain?" Thrann asked, looking up, watching his captain, "what are you looking for?"

Dolras held steady for a moment, then he raised one hand and placed it firmly on his first officer's shoulder. "Stars," he replied. "I wanted to see the stars."

CHAPTER
2

"A LITTLE MORE synthale," said Quark, DS9's Ferengi bar owner, as he hovered over Rom's shoulder.

"Don't worry, brother, I followed your instructions exactly," Rom replied, sounding annoyed but patient, at least so far, as he finished mixing the batch of cloudy green punch.

Someone has to worry, Quark thought with a mental sigh. Rom had been given a week off from his regular maintenance duties on the space station and had agreed to help out at the bar for those few days, just like old times. Already, though, Quark had begun to regret the arrangement; there was nothing worse than an employee who wasn't afraid of being fired.

"It's not that I think the Aulep are terribly picky," Quark explained, getting back to the subject at hand.

"In fact, they don't strike me as a very discriminating bunch at all. But I want everything to go right. This is too good a deal to let it get fouled up by some little detail, and I have a reputation for attention to detail."

"You do have a reputation, brother," Rom said evenly.

"What's that supposed to mean?"

"I am only agreeing with you." Rom grinned as he handed the pitcher over.

Quark wrinkled his broad, grooved nose and curled his upper lip back slightly, letting the pointed tips of his uneven teeth show. "Well, spare me," he said. He waved the punch under his nose, checking the smell, then shrugged, flipped the lid shut, and set the pitcher under the counter. He turned his back on Rom, temporarily dismissing him.

Slowly he glanced about the bar, sizing up the crowd. Quark's Place was busy but relatively peaceful for now, which was just the way he liked it. And as evening approached, it would only get busier. He always looked forward to that, to long lines at the Dabo tables and the holosuites and the bar itself, but he felt especially good whenever a lucrative acquisition was at hand—and tomorrow there would be one.

The Aulep came from an unexplored part of the Gamma Quadrant. A rather tall, thin, bony-faced race with dark orange skin, sparse black hair, and bright green-and-yellow clothes that seemed always to clash with their bodies, they had been anything but inconspicuous during their short stay on the station a few weeks ago. But the visitors had privately expressed a pressing desire to begin trading on this side of the wormhole—and trading, in particular, with Quark.

"We understand you are the one to see," Leth, the chief Aulep representative, had explained after taking a seat in a quiet corner of the bar, away from the other patrons.

"Then you are an understanding people," Quark had glibly replied, already able to smell the latinum.

"But is it true?" Leth had pressed, his long, bony face getting longer. When Quark quickly assured him it was, Leth had hinted at the broad strokes of the Aulep's trading plans and their expectations regarding Quark. But that was all. Quark had done his best to strike a deal on the spot, but all the Aulep would do in the end was agree to return in the weeks ahead and talk some more.

"I'm ready right now!" Quark had insisted.

"Good," came the reply. Then Leth had gotten up and wandered out onto the promenade, leaving Quark to sit and imagine—which, when it came to business dealings, was something he had always been very good at.

In fact, he'd been thinking about the Aulep's visit until this very day, when the Aulep were scheduled to return.

"I'll be counting on you to help out while they're

here," Quark told Rom, as his brother moved back down the bar, drawing near. "Do you think you can handle that?"

"Of course I can," Rom said resolutely. "Have I ever failed you, brother?"

"Don't start. This is serious. I've already begun brokering a possible deal. I received a communique from an Aulep representative only a few days ago."

Rom seemed clearly intrigued. Quark let him, enjoying the audience his brother provided, one he had rather missed lately, though he would never admit it. From all reports Rom was becoming a fine technician, but Quark knew only too well that Rom didn't share his brother's head for business, something Quark had never quite gotten used to. But in part because of his lack of understanding, he usually took an interest in Quark's dealings—the master at work, a glimpse at greatness, that sort of thing. Which was something Quark understood perfectly.

Rom moved around the end of the bar and took a seat directly across from Quark, then leaned closer. "So what do they have to offer?"

Quark lowered his voice. "Nothing unique. Just natural and synthetic minerals, commercial merchandise, the usual. It's the quantities I'm interested in. What seems to interest them is a few clean deals. It seems they have almost no gold-pressed latinum. I, of course, do."

"They need currency," Rom said.

"Exactly. And I intend to supply it." Quark leaned toward the nearer of his brother's very large rounded ears and lowered his voice still further. "As I under-stand it, the Aulep are willing to trade a cargo hold full of trellium crystals for gold-pressed latinum at an exchange rate of nearly two to one."

Rom nearly gasped, but this quickly turned into a conspiratorial snicker. Quark couldn't help but join in.

"Sounds almost too good to be true," Rom said.

"I know," Quark said.

"But what will you do with the crystals?"

"Ahh, well," Quark said, waving one hand at Rom, "that's the best part. As I was saying, I've already contacted, um, let's just say a special buyer, who is quite interested to say the least. Everybody wins, especially me."

Rom tipped his head in a congratulatory nod.

Quark and his brother had had their differences, some of which could not be bridged, but Rom had always given Quark credit where it was due, which was what Quark liked about him. And Quark had every intention of doing the same where Rom was concerned . . . sooner or later.

Quark let his gaze wander toward the entryway just as Lieutenant Commander Worf came in. The Klingon cut a striking figure. His long black hair, pulled back in a ponytail, the stark Klingon forehead ridges, and the trimmed black beard seemed to complement the red and black of his Starfleet uni-form. Klingons looked more natural in dark leather and metal, Quark thought, though right now he was glad there weren't any of the "natural" kind around.

Klingons had already proven to be more trouble to Quark than they were worth as customers. They were prone to violence, and it usually cost more to clean up after them than they spent. Definitely not good for business.

Worf paused to scan the room, then sat down at the far end of the bar. Alone.

"So tell me everything about these Aulep, their customs, their secret weaknesses," Rom prodded, apparently still intrigued by the depth and breadth of the upcoming deal.

Quark was less than eager to go into greater detail. "Ah—there really isn't much to tell," he said.

"What about their other trading partners? Have you made contact with any of them?"

Quark eyed Rom cautiously. He was almost too interested, as if he was fishing for trouble. "I don't know any of their other trading partners," Quark said flatly, letting his irritation show in his voice. "Not yet, anyway. They're from halfway across the Gamma Quadrant, as I said."

"I know that," Rom said. But he looked suddenly, genuinely concerned as he stared at Quark.

Quark did not enjoy the scrutiny. "What's the matter?" he asked.

"You don't know a thing about them, do you?" It wasn't a question.

"Well, not really," Quark admitted. "But I know what I need to know. More than enough to start dealing with them, and I'm a very fast learner."

"But since these Aulep are not from our part of

the galaxy, you have no idea whether you can trust them or what kinds of trading they are used to. Suppose they require the ear of your closest relative as part of the deal?"

Quark's eyes widened. He couldn't tell if Rom was joking. "Then I'd say you're lucky you have two ears."

"That's not very funny," Rom said.

"Well, you're talking nonsense."

"What I mean is, there are too many, um . . ."

Rom seemed to be searching for a word. "Variables?" Quark suggested.

"Yes, exactly."

Quark allowed himself an audible sigh. He knew what he was doing, most of the time; he'd even surprised himself now and again. Rom had apparently lost sight of that. "Have a little faith in your big brother, Rom. The truth is, I can make *any* deal work."

A commotion at the other end of the counter called their attention. Worf had gotten up again, and he was clearly displeased. He stared at the two Ferengi, and it suddenly occurred to Quark that he was simply looking for a little service—and that he probably shouldn't be kept waiting.

"Go see to Worf's needs personally," Quark told his brother, waving both hands at him, shooing him along. "All he ever wants is prune juice anyway."

A shout arose from the Dabo table. Quark watched for a moment, then relaxed when he realized it was just a Tosarian freighter crewman suddenly thrilled about his winnings . . . which, Quark trusted, would not be too large. But this was the kind of trouble he reveled in. Big winners tended to turn into big spenders, loud partiers, and holosuite junkies.

He sat back and breathed in his bar's thickly scented air, full of strange alien smells mixed with the ever-present aroma of countless spilled drinks. Yes, with a new deal in the making, it felt good to be alive.

The breath caught in his throat as Odo, the station's shapeshifting security officer, cut between patrons and headed straight for him.

"Constable!" Quark said, grinning officiously at Odo. "What can I do for you today?"

"I'm a little troubled by some of what I just overheard," Odo said. He sat down and tipped his head to one side.

Quark found his expression difficult to read. Odo's smoothed-over features and slicked-back hair lacked detail and authenticity, but they amounted to the closest version of a humanoid Odo had so far been able to accomplish. His appearance was almost comical, but Quark had learned the hard way that Odo wasn't usually joking.

"Odo, didn't anyone ever tell you it isn't polite to eavesdrop?"

"Yes, they did, unless it happens to be part of your job."

"Well, don't let it trouble you another moment. There isn't anything going on here that should concern you. Just another lovely, busy day at Quark's."

Odo's brow went up. "I think I'll decide for myself, if you don't mind. Now, tell me all about this deal you're setting up with the Aulep."

"Aulep?"

Odo nodded.

"There isn't much to tell."

"Tell me anyway."

Quark had been in this sort of conversation before. He seldom won. This time, though, he felt that he was on fairly solid ground. "It's a simple business transaction—trellium crystals for latinum, which the Aulep can get converted into whatever currency they might need. I'm doing this station a favor, you know. You should thank me. Captain Sisko has encouraged me to trade with races from the Gamma Quadrant, especially races outside the Dominion, and that's exactly what I'm doing."

Odo made a face that passed for scorn. "Perhaps," he said, "but I thought you said you don't know anything about the Aulep—what sort of people they are, who their enemies are, what their motives are, little things like that."

"And I don't have to." Quark grinned. "That's the beauty of it. Rule of acquisition number—"

"You might want to reconsider," Odo said, cutting him off. "I remember the Aulep's initial visit here a few weeks ago, including my security interview with their leader. If you'd like, I can look it up for you in my reports. As I recall, they didn't get along very well here, even though they were only on the station for a few days. Several station occupants filed complaints against them. You filed one yourself. They tried to cheat at the Dabo tables. You may recall some of this. Stop me anytime."

"Yes, yes," Quark replied, waving at the air between them as if the idea itself hung there. "A minor . . . *minor* misunderstanding, as it turned out. Once I explained the rules to them, they were fine."

"I don't believe you, Quark."

"You never do."

"And why is that?"

Quark's mood soured at Odo's patronizing grin. He sat crossing his thumbs, watching his customers. Worf sipped the drink Rom had just brought him. Garak, the station's resident Cardassian tailor, came in from the promenade with Dr. Bashir. Quark thought Garak and Bashir made an odd combination. Garak was one of the savviest beings Quark had ever encountered, with a past in Cardassian intelligence that would not bear close examination, while Julian Bashir was a bright but somewhat less initiated human with a past marked largely by academic distinction.

Unlike Cardassians and Klingons, Bashir and Garak got along just fine. The brief war between Cardassia and the Klingon Empire, and the Klingons' continued presence in this sector, had created problems for everyone. Yet the Cardassians looked more like Klingons than humans; the distinctive artery-bearing ropes of cartilage that fanned out on either side of their necks was unique, but both races possessed prominent head and facial ridges. Even their governments were similar, each featuring a long history of predominantly military rule. Nevertheless, it seemed almost no common ground existed between the two races.

Quark watched Garak and Bashir pass. They greeted Worf without incident, as he had expected.

Two Cardassian junior officers came in next, pausing as they passed by Worf, raising caution in Quark's mind. DS9 didn't get many Cardassian visitors these days, only an occasional freighter or scout ship, and many of them remained quite bitter about the Klingons' attacks on their territories.

Quark girded himself, already running a mental tab of what the damages might come to should a situation erupt. The sight of Worf's Starfleet uniform would likely help to subdue these unaccustomed visitors, but one couldn't be sure. He watched the two pause slowly behind the Klingon, where they stopped.

Worf turned and set his drink down. "Are you in need of assistance?" he asked loudly and clearly, civil but with a look that did not match his civil words.

"None," one of the Cardassian officers replied. They glanced at one another, then back to Worf. Quark tried to remind himself that Odo was standing right there, but he was relieved just the same when the two young officers moved on.

"Something troubling you, Quark?" Odo asked.

"Not a thing," Quark replied, letting himself relax. He watched the Cardassians take seats at an upper-level table.

"They make you nervous, don't they?" Odo remarked.

"No, of course not," Quark said. "Nothing to worry about. Everything is under control. And it won't be any different with the Aulep. You'll see."

"Quark, exactly where in the Gamma Quadrant is the Aulep's home planet?"

"Nowhere near the Dominion. I asked."

"I see," Odo said. "But do you have any coordinates or regional data? And are you absolutely sure the Dominion doesn't have designs on them?"

"I know what I need to know, for now," Quark said with a scowl. He didn't like the direction this conversation was taking. "As for the Dominion, why don't you go ask the Aulep?"

"I just may do that, but you're missing my point. You see, if I were going to do business with someone, I'd at least want to find out where they lived and who their enemies were."

"You don't do business," Quark said smugly. "You don't know the first thing about making a profit. You've never understood it, and you never will."

"It that so?"

"Yes."

"I could read you the summary in my file report, Quark, but what it says is that the Aulep's manner and attitudes imply a level of greed, antipathy, and general disregard for others that would make you look absolutely philanthropic."

"I'll take that as a compliment."

"Fine. Meanwhile, I trust you won't mind if I learn more about them when they arrive, and before you get yourself in too deep, I suggest you do the same. You should listen to your brother, Quark. He could be right; for all you know, you could be laundering stolen goods."

"Don't be ridiculous," Quark scoffed. "These people seem legitimate enough to me."

"Oh, well, that makes me feel *much* better," Odo said dryly, rolling his eyes.

"Well, it should. Like I said, it's a straightforward business transaction. I know that much. The rest is politics, and I try not to get involved in that. If you don't like the Aulep's manners, get someone to organize an etiquette class for them, but don't come to me—unless you need the meeting catered."

"Simple as that?" Odo said.

"Precisely. There's no need to get all worked up over everything that happens around here. Besides, when business is good, I try not to ask too many questions."

"Yes," Odo said, smiling sidelong at Quark, "I'm well aware of that."

Quark let his scowl deepen.

Rom came back and started fixing drinks for another order. Quark instantly took the opportunity to join him on the other side of the counter. "You'll need a hand with those," he said, selecting two clean glasses, setting them up.

Rom looked up, surprised. "I will?"

"Yes, you will."

"Why, thank you, brother."

Quark avoided Odo's gaze as he collected a tray. "Don't mention it," he muttered.

"Is anything wrong?" Rom asked Odo, pausing.

Odo stood up. "No," he said, turning to leave, "not yet."

CHAPTER
3

CAPTAIN BENJAMIN SISKO, Federation commander of DS9, sat motionless in his chair, elbows on his desktop, dark-skinned fingers steepled just below his chin, listening as Odo delivered his daily station security status briefing: an Andorian had been caught shoplifting on the Promenade; a Bajoran boy had gone missing for several hours, only to be found napping in one of the cargo bays; the crew of a scientific research vessel had resisted Odo's initial efforts to examine their delicate cargo until he threatened to slap them all in quarantine—and there had been two fistfights.

Odo mentioned the Aulep last.

"Yes," Sisko said, "I remember them."

"What was your impression of them?"

"They seemed innocuous enough, as far as I can recall. Is there a problem?"

Odo nodded. "Quark is apparently attempting to orchestrate a trade agreement with them."

Sisko let his chin bob on his fingertips. That sounded fine. "I'm glad to hear it. That's one of the reasons I like having him around."

"Yes, but unfortunately he's going about it in typical Ferengi fashion. He's completely in the dark about these people, and so are we. They're due back today. I just wanted to let you know."

"I'm sure the trade agreement will be all right, but keep an eye on them."

"I'll do that," Odo said, sounding satisfied.

Good, Sisko thought, considering the matter sufficiently tended to . . . for now. Odo was perhaps the most capable security officer he had ever served with, and his instincts were seldom wrong, which made his concerns something not to be dismissed.

"What were you telling me earlier about a fight among the Ridorians?" Sisko asked.

Odo breathed a tired sigh. "They walk everywhere in a column, arranged according to height. A little while ago, two of them got into a disagreement over a centimeter."

"I see."

"Finally I offered to shorten one of them and stretch the other."

Sisko held back his chuckle. His comm badge chirped before he could say anything else.

"Kira to Captain Sisko," the voice of his Bajoran first officer announced.

Sisko tapped his badge. "Yes, Major."

"Are you forgetting something, sir? Your son has been waiting in one of the runabouts for almost an hour now. I'm afraid he's going to start without you."

"Ah, yes," Sisko replied, raising his lean yet considerable mass out of the chair. He usually had too many things on his plate and never enough time to get to them all, but it was a situation his son, like his crew, were used to. "Thank you, Major. Tell him I'll be right there."

"Yes, sir," Kira said.

"I wasn't aware you and Jake were leaving the station," Odo said. "I didn't mean to keep you."

"Oh, we're not going anywhere in particular," Sisko said. "I haven't filed a flight plan."

Odo looked puzzled. "Then why is Jake waiting in a runabout?"

"Because he wants what every boy his age has wanted for hundreds of years."

"And what is that?"

Sisko grinned as he came around his desk and brushed past Odo. "He wants to learn how to drive."

Sisko made his way straight to the runabout landing pads, where he found his son Jake already sitting at the controls of the *Rio Grande,* almost bouncing in the seat. Sisko could hardly blame him.

As he had entered his mid-teens, Jake had grown into as fine a young man as Sisko and his late wife, Jennifer, could have hoped for. He was every bit his father's son. Dark skin and hair, strong features, gentle eyes, and a smile that always seemed to work . . . even on his father. And Jake had compassion, something Sisko thought might be as important as a career with Starfleet—which was the one thing he and Jake seemed at odds about.

Of course, the Academy wasn't the only future, not even for the son of a Starfleet captain. Although Jake had stated his desire to explore a different path, there remained the possibility of his one day attending Starfleet Academy. At least, Sisko liked to think so. Right now, however, Jake was spending a lot of time looking ahead, another consequence of his age, and something Sisko was glad to encourage. Overall, Jake's studies were going well, as was his writing; he was revising a new story about a retired Starfleet officer who teaches an alien culture to play baseball—Jake's favorite sport, as well as his father's. Sisko had read a draft, and in his opinion, the work was definitely improving.

And at the moment Jake was most interested in learning to pilot a runabout, or at least gaining enough knowledge to allow him to bring one safely home should his life come to depend on it . . . again.

He'd been lucky the first time, but being stranded in a disabled runabout on the other side of the wormhole was not something Jake or his father wanted to see happen again. Sisko had agreed that a few lessons were probably a good idea. The only problem was trying to make the time.

"You look excited," Sisko remarked as he sat in the left seat.

Jake's broad grin was irrepressible. "Who wouldn't be?" he said. "I finally get to *do* something."

"There's plenty to do around the station," Sisko said.

"And all of it boring, compared to this, especially with Nog away. A guy needs a little adventure once in a while."

"A little excitement," Sisko agreed.

"Right. New challenges," Jake said.

"Exactly!" Sisko grinned. "How's that chair feel?"

Jake glanced nervously about. "Shouldn't I be in it?"

Sisko chuckled. "You can stay there, and I'll take Ops. Eventually we can switch. We're going to have to take this a step a time. Do you think you're ready?"

"You know I am."

"I guess I do," Sisko said. He knew Jake had been studying every system on the station's runabouts for weeks now, learning all that he could—the kind of knowledge one needed to man the Ops station, in particular, though he had studied conn as well. And he had spent considerable time in a specially programed holosuite flight simulation, which had gone a long way toward making a good classroom pilot out of him. Sisko didn't doubt his son's basic readiness to sit in either chair, and despite some nervousness, Jake seemed confident enough. But this was the moment that mattered. Some things were best learned by doing. Hands-on. Trial-and-error.

"You know what you always say," Jake said, turning slightly to face the main control panel, touching lighted pads to bring some of the runabout's main systems online. "Learning is constant."

"Do I say that?"

Jake just smiled at his father.

Sisko tipped his head to one side, playing along. "What else do I say?"

"You say that reason we're out here is to learn."

"Do I?"

Jake nodded.

Sisko knew he had given that speech often enough: live and learn—or was it the other way around? That was why human beings were in space—to seek, to explore, to discover. And that was why Jake was sitting in the pilot seat of a runabout.

Sisko opened a channel. "Rio Grande to Ops, we're ready for departure," he said, checking communications as he did so. Jake was busy running his own systems checks and doing a fine job so far.

"You're cleared," Major Kira replied. "Outer system flight path logged. Good luck, and have fun."

"Thank you, Major." Sisko glanced to his right. He found Jake looking back at him and saw what he thought was just the right balance of anxiety, confidence, and pure enthusiasm in the boy's bright eyes.

Sisko let a gentle smile find his lips. "I believe we'll have plenty of both."

Jake waited patiently, a runner at the starting line.

"Go ahead," Sisko said. "Take her out."

The engines hummed as the runabout lifted off the landing pad on DS9's habitat ring. Jake was obviously tense, but he managed to get the ship away and clear of the station smoothly enough.

"Now you're going to ease the power up," Sisko said. "First, what's your heading?"

Jake glanced down. "Zero zero zero mark five."

"Good. Now get us up to speed, but watch the power balance. The computer should keep the engines aligned, but you'll want to keep an eye on it."

"I know," Jake said.

"Good."

Jake accelerated to one-quarter impulse. He kept their course steady. Sisko watched with satisfaction as Jake concentrated intensely on the glowing blue, white, and crimson readings displayed at his fingertips. At eighty kilometers out from Bajor they passed through the Denorius asteroid belt, and Sisko watched with ever increasing pride as Jake gently wove a path through the loose assortment of rocks and boulders.

Then, in the void between the Bajoran system's fourth and fifth planets, Sisko sat back. "Why don't you try to experiment a little?" he said. "Have some fun with it!" He gave Jake an encouraging nod.

He gulped when the ship lurched under them as Jake attempted his first free turn, working the inertia dampeners a little too hard, but the second try went much more smoothly, and Sisko forced himself to relax.

The system's largest gas giant lay just ahead. Jake seemed to take the huge gravity-well in stride, adjusting course as the computer lit the appropriate navigation display. Though Jake grew noticeably more nervous as the pull of the multicolored Jupiter-like world made itself known, Sisko let him meet the challenge, remaining a simple observer. He heard Jake breathe a sigh as the enormous planet passed by without incident.

Sisko didn't say a word. Not bad, he thought to himself.

"I'm going to put her through a few rolls and spirals," Jake said, straight-faced.

Sisko looked at him, and as he expected, Jake broke into a chuckle.

"Maybe next time," Sisko said, shaking his head. Cute, he thought. "We don't want you getting carried away. I'd say you've done your homework, though. We'll have you flying at warp speeds in no time."

"Thanks, but for now I'll be happy when I can do this part a little better."

"Uh-huh. And I think I know why."

Jake's eyes stayed with the controls. "What do you mean?"

"I was just thinking about a certain recent Bajoran visitor, a girl by the name of . . . Elliena, isn't it?"

Jake remained silent. That silence, Sisko thought, spoke volumes. The girl was about Jake's age, bright, attractive, the daughter of a Bajoran diplomat who represented the planet's Natural Resource Council. DS9 had been helping the Bajorans coordinate a planet-wide studying to determine fully what shape Bajor was really in, following the long ecologically and geologically devastating Cardassian occupation. The consul, his wife, and their daughter had been to the station several times in the past two months, giving Jake and Elliena more than enough time to get to know each other pretty well. Fine people, all of them, Sisko had decided. And more than welcome.

"You're not getting serious about Elliena, are you?" Sisko asked, pressing a little.

Jake squirmed. "Maybe. I don't know. It depends on what you mean by 'serious'?"

"Oh, I don't know exactly, but if you start making plans to attend whatever Bajoran university she's planning to attend, I hope you'll let me know."

Jake looked up, a glow on his face. "Okay, I will. But for now I'd just like to wait and see what happens, and maybe take her out for a firsthand look at her own solar system." He nodded toward the window. "She's never seen any of this for herself."

"Take Elliena on a flight?" Sisko said, raising his eyebrows at the boy. "Just the two of you?" That sounded rather romantic, actually.

"Once I'm approved, of course," Jake added.

"Of course. And I'd say all you need is a little practice. Actually, you're doing fine."

"I hope I do as well with Elliena."

Sisko chuckled. He was just getting used to having a son who was dating. He and Jake both had a lot to learn, but that would never change.

He focused once more on the control console. "Let's see if you can bring her around to mark fifteen," he said. He watched his son execute the course correction exactly, then said, "You know, Jake, it sounds as if you think that women are a lot harder to handle than runabouts."

"I didn't mean that, exactly."

"I know."

A comet came into view to port. Sisko made mention of it, but Jake seemed to spot it at the same time. He paced the comet for a time, then, at Sisko's urging, changed to a course that would allow them to pass through its tail. As the runabout drew nearer, it encountered the comet's slight gravitational pull. Ice and dust particles swirled about them, just beyond the ship's twin observation windows. Jake worked at the controls to smooth their course and acceleration again.

"You're thinking about a lot more than just sight-seeing, aren't you?" Sisko said, watching Jake as the runabout continued on its way.

Jake nodded. "Elliena would love to see this, don't you think?" he said, as he looked out into the comet's tail.

"Yes, I do."

"I'd be glad to help you in any way I can," Sisko said. "That is, if you want me to. But if you're anything like me, most of what I tell you is going to go in one ear and out the other. The truth is, like piloting, relationships are an area where experience is one of the best teachers."

Jake sighed, then added a grin. "Don't I know it!"

The shuttle's comm chirped, followed by the voice of Lieutenant Commander Worf.

"Go ahead," Sisko answered.

"Captain, you asked to be informed when the Aulep arrived. They have just come through the wormhole and are maneuvering into docking position now."

"Thank you."

"Captain," Worf added, "the Aulep are asking to speak with you as soon as possible. They insist I inform them as to where and when that will be. Flenn, their mission commander, says the matter is quite urgent."

"What matter is that?"

"Unclear. He indicated an interest in establishing better relations with the Federation. Nothing more."

"Doesn't sound all that urgent," Jake commented, keeping his voice just above a whisper.

"No, it does not," Worf answered, his tone implying a certain level of annoyance with the subject.

Sisko gathered from this that the Aulep had already managed to leave a mixed impression. Still, he would keep an open mind. After all, most people had good reasons for acting the way they did. He doubted the Aulep's situation was unusual, but sometimes, he thought, looking at Jake, even little things could seem much more important to one person than they did to others.

In any case, he wasn't in a position to take anything or anyone associated with the Gamma Quadrant less than seriously.

"Very well. Tell him something will be arranged as soon as I return. Sisko out." He turned to Jake. The lesson was about to be cut short, and there was nothing he could do about it. It was the sort of thing that happened too often between them, but Sisko was getting better at making it up to Jake, and he thought Jake was getting better at understanding why it happened.

"Think you can take us home?" he asked.

Jake nodded. "Yes, sir."

"We'll make time for another lesson soon, I promise." He put his hand on Jake's shoulder.

"I know." Raising his hand, Jake gripped his father's fingers briefly, then he returned his attention to the console.

Sisko watched Jake take the runabout through a slow turn out in the middle of nowhere. They had been here before, he realized, in a hand-built Bajoran light-sail spacecraft, and in the process they had repeated a piece of history, discovering the truth in the ancient Bajoran legends.

"Steady as she goes," Sisko said, as the *Rio Grande* straightened and began its trek home.

CHAPTER
4

SISKO FOUND THREE visitors waiting for him in his office when he arrived back at DS9. The Aulep greeted him with smiles that looked strikingly humanoid. They were a bit short, none more than five feet tall, and their orange skin and garish clothing hurt Sisko's eyes almost as much as they offended his fashion sense. Were the Aulep color-blind?

One of the three stepped forward and extended a small but thickly boned hand. Sisko took the hand and shook it firmly. The alien's grip was strong, but the flesh was smooth. And what was that sweet, almost perfumelike odor?

Odo stood silently by, keeping them company. Sisko exchanged glances with his security chief, found solidarity in the other's eyes, then turned his full attention to the Aulep.

"I'm Captain Sisko. Welcome to *Deep Space Nine.*"

"Flenn," the other said. "I am fascinated by this custom of yours."

Sisko decided Flenn meant the handshake. "It's an old one."

"Intended to assure others that you hold no weapons, I assume," Flenn suggested.

"I suppose that might have something to do with it."

"Quite sensible, I think," Flenn said. "There are many things about this station, and about Starfleet, which impress me already, and I have only a little knowledge. Of course with your help, that will change."

"I intend to be as helpful as possible," Sisko said.

"Then the future looks bright, wouldn't you agree?"

"Most of the time," Sisko said, sensing a need for increased caution, finding the Aulep's manner perhaps too ingratiating.

Up close, the Aulep had a rather leathery complexion, accented by a darkening of the skin along their broad cheekbones, their prominent chins, and the ridge where human eyebrows would have been. The eyes themselves, deep red and unblinking, glistened with moisture and at first gave an impression of innocence. Sisko remembered this from his brief meeting with these same Aulep some time ago. He reminded himself how deceptive visual impressions could be.

Sisko sat on the front corner of his desk. "I understand you want to talk about diplomatic relations. What sort of arrangements do you have in mind?"

"To begin with," Flenn said, "we are interested in forming a limited alliance."

"And why is that?" Odo asked. He glanced at Sisko, as if to ask belated permission to speak. Sisko nodded once.

"We have many reasons," Flenn replied.

"Of course you do," Odo said, looking to Sisko again.

"Which are?" Sisko sensed that the answer might be harder to get at than expected.

"Do you want me to list them?" Flenn asked, losing just a bit of his amiable manner.

"That would be fine," Odo said.

"I came to speak with Captain Sisko," Flenn said, turning away from Odo and folding his arms.

Sisko's brow went up. The Aulep clearly had secrets. "I see. But Odo makes a valid point. It will be necessary for us to learn a good deal more about you and your people, your history, your culture, your neighbors—and for you in turn to learn about the Federation—before we get to that stage. Are you at war?"

"At war?" Flenn said, making a tight face. "Certainly not."

"Are you planning to be?" Odo asked.

"No," Flenn said instantly. "You speak as if we were part of some offensive armada."

43

"And why would we think that?" Sisko asked.

"We understand your concern, of course," Flenn said, "but you needn't worry."

Sisko was beginning to see something of an evasive pattern in Flenn's responses. "You know, we have no idea exactly where you're from," he said.

"A distant sector of the Gamma Quadrant," Flenn replied. "I thought that had been established. It makes little difference at the moment."

"It might," Sisko said. "You see, I was thinking in terms of coordinates."

Flenn glanced at both his companions, who said nothing but seemed to communicate on some level all the same. Sisko had the feeling this was not uncommon.

"Captain," Flenn said, "any information you desire will eventually be given. But for now we do not need the coordinates of your Earth in order to meet or negotiate with you; we do not require the Federation's historical or cultural résumé or your own personal history. Most of that, we believe, is your business. And we trust that as information is required, you will supply it."

"That is a very pragmatic approach," Sisko said.

"Thank you. We are interested in the present and, most importantly, in the future. No disrespect is intended, Captain, but is such an approach beyond your abilities?"

Odo opened his mouth to respond, but Sisko held one hand up, staying the words. He turned and stared at Flenn, silent, unblinking, considering the other's words. He watched Flenn's big red eyes; somehow they didn't seem nearly so innocuous now. In fact, the longer he and Flenn stood staring at each other, the more nervous the alien seemed to get, as if he'd placed a bet and was waiting for the wheel of chance to stop its spin.

"That's just it," Sisko finally said, "you never really know."

Flenn seemed to stumble over this, though he said nothing. Sisko decided to treat Flenn's last question as an honest one and not sarcasm.

"However," he went on, "I think we can probably get started."

Flenn blinked several times. "Good. Very good."

The mood in the office seemed to soften. Sisko went around behind his deck and sat down. He motioned the Aulep to chairs on either side of him and Odo, but the visitor seemed content to stand.

"What would you suggest?" Sisko asked.

"I've given that much thought," Flenn replied, apparently pleased to have the meeting back on track. "Perhaps you would agree to join us for dinner aboard our ship—say, in an hour. We can discuss this at greater length. Your trade ambassador has already agreed to be there. I'm sure the meeting will be productive."

Sisko cocked his head. "Our . . . trade ambassador?"

Flenn nodded. "Yes, Ambassador Quark."

"Ah, yes, of course. Ambassador Quark." Sisko shook his head, then did his best to contain a snicker as he glanced to one side and encountered Odo's scowl. "As a matter of fact," he said, "I wouldn't miss it."

Sisko stepped off DS9's docking ring and into the Aulep vessel a few minutes late, only to learn that Quark would apparently be later still. The Aulep commander seemed to take this all in stride. Sisko followed Flenn and his two companions down several dark, narrow corridors, until they emerged suddenly into brightness.

The dining quarters aboard Flenn's ship were magnificent, and tinged with the sweet perfume-like smell of the Aulep themselves, mixed with the promising aroma of unseen foods.

Rich, lavishly embroidered tapestries covered the ceiling, while the walls were done in finely detailed murals, most depicting a much greater banquet hall. Dozens of extravagantly dressed Aulep had been painted into the scenes, all of them enjoying a bountiful feast. The painting, combined with the rich aroma of whatever was cooking nearby, made Sisko feel as if he were actually there himself, in the mural, about to participate in the feast.

Highly polished golden rails ran throughout the room, all firmly affixed to the walls and deck; the center rail passed by the main table.

"Beautiful, aren't they?" Flenn said, apparently noticing Sisko's stare. He placed one stout little hand on the rail nearest him. "A holdover from an earlier time. An elegant means of getting around or steadying oneself, from before the modern age of artificial gravity and inertia dampeners."

"You keep them as part of a tradition, then," Sisko said.

"More or less. There is no longer a need for them, which is why they are considered fashionable, of course."

"Vanity," Sisko said.

"Yes," Flenn said without hesitation.

Sisko nodded understanding as he continued to look around.

The table itself was pure white. Under its glasslike surface clouds of light-colored mist swirled about, the whole thing reminding Sisko of a piece from a giant crystal ball.

"You must do very well, economically."

"I assure you we do," Flenn said, grinning. Then, apparently sensing the seriousness of Sisko's mood, he asked, "Does this concern you?"

"Not necessarily. Tell me, do all your people share in that wealth, or is it reserved for a select few, as you?"

"Many are well off, some are not—as in any other universe. The division of wealth will always be unequal, certainly. I'm sure it is no different on your world."

"That is something we ought to talk about. Many worlds in the Federation have overcome that problem."

47

Flenn stared at Sisko for a moment, straight-faced, then a hint of the smile returned. "Ah! You are joking. I understand."

"I wasn't joking."

Flenn's expression soured abruptly, bringing darker coloring to the raised, already darkened areas of his face. Sisko watched him glance briefly at his two companions again, then turn back. "In that case, you are apparently talking in circles. Testing us somehow. Which means you are trying to spoil this pleasant occasion, I think, and for no clear reason. Am I mistaken?"

"I assure you that I mean no insult, and I make no judgments. I'm simply stating a fact."

They eyed each other for a moment, and Sisko sensed the tension was not so great as it had seemed. The Aulep were easily incensed, but their ire ran shallow.

"Perhaps we do need to clarify a few points," Flenn said.

"I'll be honest," Sisko told him. "I tend to have certain personal reservations about anyone who regards status and pretense too highly. However, that does not mean we can't make considerable progress in planning future Federation-Aulep relations. I can certainly see why you and Quark have been able to get along, though. The Ferengi are as acquisitive a species as I have ever encountered."

"We were under the impression that most Federation races were like the Ferengi," Flenn said.

That doesn't surprise me in the least, Sisko thought. He cleared his throat, but held his tongue.

"I trust I haven't missed anything!" Quark said as he hurriedly entered the room, practically on cue.

"We were just discussing how well suited you are to working with the Aulep," Sisko said. "In fact, I'm thinking of asking you to volunteer your services as official liaison between *Deep Space Nine* and the Aulep people . . . uh, Mr. Ambassador."

Sisko held Quark's gaze. The Ferengi hardly skipped a beat. "I—I'd be honored, of course, Captain," he said. "It's the least I can do."

"Good. I'll let the two of you start discussing your trade interests soon. But in the interest of clarification, the three of us should spend some time discussing Aulep culture, as well as some of the Federation's more prominent races—just to get to know each other. Nothing you don't feel comfortable with, of course. And perhaps you will tell me about your goals. You are interested in more than trade, I assume."

"That is true, Captain," Flenn said, falling in line now and easily keeping pace. "We would like to enter into a formal arrangement with your Federation. A limited alliance. One that we believe might ultimately benefit many worlds on both sides of the wormhole."

"That is an admirable purpose, but I have to wonder exactly why such an alliance is important to you."

"We like to do business with friends."

"Speaking of friends," Sisko said, "how would such an arrangement affect your relations with other races in the Gamma Quadrant?"

"You needn't be concerned about that," Flenn said hastily and rather flatly.

Sisko looked at him. "No?"

"No."

"Tell me, is the Dominion a threat to you?" Sisko asked outright.

"No," Flenn said again, clearly growing agitated. "Fortunately, they are a long way off."

Sisko still didn't have the information he was after. "Then tell me, exactly how far is 'a long way off'?"

"Oh, Captain, you're always worried about what the neighbors will think," Quark said, stepping between them. He turned to Flenn. "He's like that. All hu-mans are. You get used to it." Quark slapped his hands together and rubbed them briskly. "I think we should move on."

"Of course," Flenn said. "Let's eat, shall we?"

Two more Aulep, one of them female, entered the dining room carrying large polished trays laden with steaming bowls. The aroma reminded Sisko of stewed tomatoes.

"I do a little cooking myself," Sisko said as Flenn led the way to the table.

"Let me know what you like, and we'll see that you get the recipes," Flenn said as he showed Sisko to a well-padded chair. The first bowls contained some kind of soup, a light brownish broth rich with chunks of unfamiliar but tender vegetables. Sisko leaned forward and sniffed, savoring the smell and the moist warmth of the steam rising to his face. He really was hungry.

Before he could reach for his spoon, however, his comm badge chirped.

"Kira to Sisko."

DS9's Bajoran first officer was on duty in Ops; she knew Sisko was having dinner with their visitors and that he didn't want to be interrupted, so he was fairly certain whatever she wanted wouldn't bring a smile to his face.

"Go ahead, Major," he said.

"An unidentified vessel just came through the wormhole. Their weapons systems are powered up, and they're not answering our hails."

"Go to yellow alert. What's their bearing?"

"They appear to be heading for *Deep Space Nine.*"

"Mr. Worf," Sisko said, "raise the shields and be sure to extend them to protect all ships docked at the station."

"We already have," Worf said, his deep voice a sudden contrast to Kira's.

Sisko felt his appetite vanish. "Mr. Worf, what is their capability?"

"Their weapons appear formidable enough to present a threat, Captain."

"Very well, arm our weapons," Sisko told the Klingon.

"Weapons armed," Worf said a moment later. "I am reading their shields at maximum."

"I have them on visual," Kira said. "And, Captain . . ."

"What is it, Major?"

"This ship is slightly smaller than the Aulep vessel you are now aboard, but it's similar in design."

Sisko looked at Flenn, narrowing his eyes. "How similar?" he asked.

"Nearly identical," Worf answered for her.

"Stand by." Sisko fixed Flenn with a hard stare. "Friends of yours?"

"Captain," Flenn said, wearing his virtuous expression again, "I assure you, I have no idea—"

"I don't need that kind of assurance. I need to know what's going on."

"Captain," Kira interrupted, "the new arrival is hailing the Aulep ship, but there has been no response so far."

"Is something wrong with your communications system?" Sisko asked accusingly.

"Not that I know of," Flenn said, waving to one of the other Aulep, who got up instantly and left the dining room. "But I ask you, Captain, would it be prudent to respond to someone when we don't know who that someone is?"

"Why shouldn't you, unless you aren't telling me the whole truth?"

"We have done nothing, Captain."

Sisko leaned toward Flenn, who was seated on his

right. "Other than suggest an alliance with the Federation. But an alliance against whom, I now wonder?"

"Captain, you have no right to assume—"

"I'm sure I do," Sisko boomed, less than gracious now. He didn't like being played for a fool. "What were you saying about not being at war with anyone?"

"It was the truth!" Flenn was doing his best to look wounded.

Sisko wasn't buying it. "Take us to your bridge."

"That is not possible just now, Captain," Flenn said, sounding almost as if he was in pain. "We are not ready to allow you into sensitive areas."

"We've allowed you into ours."

"As is your prerogative, of course."

"Then," Sisko said, measuring his tone, "take us to your observation deck. Unless you have a problem with that."

"Very well. This way." Flenn headed for the door with suddenly heavy feet.

"Shall I wait here?" Quark asked, a look of nervous innocence on his face—a look he was uniquely good at.

"Not a chance," Sisko said.

Flenn led the way back out into the dark corridors while Sisko and Quark followed. The walk was a short one and ended in a plain gray-walled room half the size of the one they had just left. Flenn touched a button and the wall ahead of them became transparent.

Sisko found himself gazing out into space, past the leading edge of the nearest of DS9's tall, arching docking pylons, toward the dark region of space where the wormhole lay. The unidentified vessel hung in space, silent and stationary now, only a few thousand kilometers away—waiting for something, it seemed. A stout cylindrical ship several times the size of a runabout, with a wide wedge-shaped structure dominating the top, it had two long tubes underneath that curved back around the tail and ultimately joined the wedge.

Indeed, Sisko thought, the ship looked almost precisely like Flenn's. He tapped his comm badge again. "Any luck hailing them?" he asked.

"None," Kira said.

"Keep trying. I don't want a firefight at such close range. There are too many ships around the docking ring. I'm trying to get some answers on this end. Sisko out."

He turned to face the others.

"I swear I don't know a thing!" Quark quickly assured the captain as their eyes met.

"Well, somebody must," Sisko said.

"In our region of space, there are many ships similar to ours, Captain," Flenn said. "We can't know the mind of every—"

"Captain," Worf interrupted, "the intruder is now targeting the ship you are on."

54

"Very well, Flenn," Sisko said sternly, stepping closer to his host, bending slightly, leaving only a few centimeters of space between the two of them. He pointed toward the ship beyond the viewport. "I am running out of patience. For the last time, who are they, and what do they want?"

CHAPTER
5

"WE REALLY DON'T know who they are—at least, not exactly," Flenn hedged, obviously growing uneasy.

Sisko wasn't in the mood. Not when his station was being threatened. He was more than a head taller than the Aulep, and as he loomed over Flenn, he used every bit of his height and mass to intimidate the mission commander.

"Explain 'not exactly,'" he demanded.

Flenn looked to Quark, but the Ferengi only gave the Aulep commander a shrug in return. Sisko found the brief exchange most interesting.

"Captain," Worf's voice said from Sisko's comm badge, "the alien vessel is firing."

Worf's words were followed by a heavy, booming shudder that resonated through the docking ring, then through the hull of the Aulep ship. Sisko looked out through the observation wall in time to see two more bright greenish white flashes erupt from the unidentified ship. He felt both impacts just as a series of bright, lingering flashes lit up the space between them. The intruder might be well armed, but DS9 was better protected.

"Shields holding, down seven percent," Worf said.

"Captain," Kira's voice said, "they appear to be firing directly at the Aulep ship."

"Confirmed," Worf said.

"They must realize we have shields in place," Sisko replied.

"The attack appears designed to weaken the shields around the Aulep vessel."

"Captain," Worf said, "I recommend we get you out of there immediately."

Sisko felt inclined to agree as another series of flashes caught his eye. The station's shields lit up with sparkling colors as the last burst was dispersed, but the kinetic energy of the blasts made the walls rattle and the deck shake hard enough to upset his balance.

A brief silence followed.

"They've ceased firing," Worf reported. "Sir, I believe they are recharging their weapons for the next attack. Request permission to return fire."

"Hold off." He needed a minute to think, and since the station didn't seem to be in immediate danger, he intended to take it. No sense rushing into something he might later regret.

Slowly he turned. He wasn't through with Flenn just yet.

"Do you still have an open channel to the attacking ship?" he asked.

"Yes," Kira said, "but there's no response."

"Let's assume they're listening. Tell them that if they do not end this attack, we will be forced to retaliate. They may not realize how well armed we are. If there's no change, you're authorized to fire a warning shot, but hold direct fire until I give the order. Meanwhile, keep me informed."

Flenn stood with his hands folded, a look of mild surprise on his darkened orange features. "Captain, I know how this looks, but I can see you are a man of restraint, intuition, and compassion. I would like to thank you—"

"You would be in the middle of a dogfight in open space right now if it were not for *Deep Space Nine!*" Sisko snapped, his voice hard. "You might even be dead. Think about that."

"Captain, I take exception to your tone," Flenn said, indignant. "And in any case, we are quite capable of defending ourselves."

"You might yet have the opportunity to do just that, because if I don't start getting some honest answers out of you, I will ask you and your ship to leave this station, for safety purposes. Our safety, not yours."

"I protest, Captain!" Flenn said, souring further. "We are the victims here, just as you are."

"Why don't we ask your attackers about that?"

"The intruder's weapons are fully powered again," Worf informed Sisko.

"We should take Worf's advice and evacuate this ship," Quark said nervously. "After all, we aren't accomplishing anything."

Sisko stopped Quark with a cold stare. "No one is going anywhere until I find out who is shooting at us and why."

Another series of shots struck in rapid succession, illuminating the shields with a blinding brightness once more. With the last volley the Aulep ship suddenly bucked, then shuddered. Sisko steadied himself against the wall as Quark and Flenn picked themselves up off the floor. Alarms sounded from somewhere in the ceiling.

Sisko slapped his comm badge. "Report!"

"Sir," Worf responded, "the last of those shots buckled a narrow section of our shields and struck the Aulep vessel. The docking clamps are badly damaged, and we have a hull breach in the docking ring. We've already contained the breach with a forcefield. I have fired a phaser burst across the intruder's bow, and we are continuing to repeat our hails, but there is still no response."

"Shield integrity has been reestablished," Kira said. "Shield capacity down seventeen percent overall but holding."

Worf said, "Request permission to return fire, sir!"

"Wait!" Sisko said.

"Captain," Quark pleaded, "you've got to do something! Why don't you let Worf blast them?"

"I'm scanning the damage to the Aulep ship," Major Kira said. "There's a hull breach, but I'd say the ship itself is in no immediate danger."

"You may want to check with your crew," Sisko told Flenn, who was already tapping at a terminal mounted on the wall behind him. An instant later the door slid open and several Aulep rushed in. They huddled with Flenn for a moment, apparently upset. They kept their voices low so he couldn't make out their words.

"Any casualties?" Sisko asked.

Flenn turned to him once more. "No. Fortunately no one has been injured. However, there is considerable damage to the hull, as your officer informed us. Our main cargo bay has been ripped open. The area is now sealed off, and we are attempting to assess the full extent of the breach."

One of the attending Aulep suddenly pointed, directing everyone's attention once more to the observation wall. A quickly dispersing cloud of debris could be seen floating away from the Aulep ship and the station. Flenn seemed to take an intense interest in it.

Before anyone could comment, the intruder fired yet again, lighting up the stations's shields and jostling the ship's occupants once more. The shields seemed to hold. The Aulep rushed back into their loose huddle, whispering, though only for a moment.

"Captain," Flenn said, turning and looking nearly as pallid as Quark now, though in an entirely different shade. "If I may correct myself, we have determined who the attackers are, but we do not know much about them or their motives. In any case, we feel that Quark is right and you must do something to stop them. At once."

Another blast shook the ship, but this time no more damage was done. Finally Sisko nodded. This had gone on long enough, and clearly he wasn't going to learn more from Flenn right now.

"Agreed, but we're not done yet." He tapped his comm badge. "Sisko to Worf. End the attack by any means necessary."

He listened as Major Kira sent a final request to the intruders to power down their weapons. Another burst flashed from the intruder's bow and struck DS9's shields once more in the same spot. So much for tact and diplomacy, he thought.

The bright red-and-white beam of the station's powerful phasers flashed into view as it struck the intruder with perfect accuracy. Worf fired a second time, and Sisko watched the target ship's shields glow brightly, then go dark. A third beam struck the hull, causing a small explosion along the ship's extended stern, which was easily visible from his position aboard Flenn's vessel.

"Their shields are down, and their propulsion

system is off-line," Worf reported. "The target has been neutralized."

"Hail now being acknowledged, Captain," Kira said. "They would like to speak to whoever is in charge."

"Let them stand by for a moment." Sisko tapped his comm badge, closing the link as he turned to Flenn. He found his host already engaged in a discussion with yet another contingent of his crew, three uniformed Aulep officers who had entered as the first group was leaving.

"I am needed on my bridge, Captain," Flenn said after a pause. "It is urgent."

"Very well," Sisko said. "Let's all go. Now that we're getting to be such good friends, I'm sure you won't mind."

"Actually, Captain—"

"Excellent. Coming, Quark?" Sisko asked, starting out of the room.

"I'm going where you're going," Quark replied, falling into step at Sisko's heels.

Flenn seemed to sigh in resignation.

Out in the corridor Sisko let Flenn take the lead. They moved quickly along the darkened hallway, then up a ramp, through a pair of automatic doors, and into a small but brightly lit control room that had to be the Aulep bridge.

The room was well organized, and the level of technology was admirable, even at a glance. Five crew members—three male, two female—occupied lushly padded chairs that rested on long pneumatic arms. As the technicians worked, the chairs moved them deftly from one set of control panels to another. Bright metal panels covered most of the nonessential surfaces.

"Major Kira," Sisko said, tapping his comm badge again as he watched a large screen set into one of the bridge consoles. "Can you patch that other ship's signal through to the Aulep bridge?"

"Tell the Aulep to open a channel," Kira replied.

Sisko looked at a dour-faced Flenn, who hesitated for a very long moment, then signaled one of his bridge crew to comply. The technician nodded and tapped at his console.

"Go ahead, Major," Sisko said. "Put them on."

The face that appeared on the screen was that of a male alien almost identical to Flenn and his crew members, except that his skin was darker and slightly brownish. Even his clothing was somewhat similar to Flenn's, though the colors, mostly tans and light greens, were not so garish.

"I thought you didn't know them," Sisko said, folding his arms and glaring at Flenn, who said not a word.

"Captain," Quark said, shaking his head. "I—"

Sisko motioned him to silence, then addressed the alien on the screen. "I am Captain Benjamin Sisko. Why have you fired on this station?"

"I am Dorram, Commanding the Rylep vessel *Toshien*," the alien replied. "And the answer to your question should be obvious: I demand to know why the Aulep are being afforded protection by you and your station."

"I recommend you destroy the attackers while you have the chance," Flenn said softly, moving closer to Sisko. "You've seen how hostile they can be."

"I don't think you're in a position to make demands, or recommendations," Sisko said loudly. "Either of you."

"Captain," Dorram continued, clearly agitated, "we have a right to know why have you allied yourselves with the Aulep."

Sisko found a similar expression on Flenn's face as he compared the two. They could have been brothers. "This station is available to any race that wishes to make use of it," he told the Rylep. "I intend to protect it and anyone who docks at it in good faith—which, by the way, is a privilege that can be revoked." He cast a grave look in Flenn's direction. "If you have a legitimate grievance against the Aulep, I'd be glad to listen, since they don't seem terribly eager to talk about it. But until I get all the facts—"

"We will give you all the facts you need," Dorram said.

"Don't believe anything they say, Captain!" Flenn said. "The Rylep are a treacherous people."

"Not so treacherous as the Aulep," Dorram replied.

"I see," Sisko said. He turned to the Ferengi. "Quark, any insight here?"

"Again, I assure you, Captain," Quark replied, breaking a rather unusual spell of silence. "I don't know anything about these Rylep. Nothing at all!"

"I have a suggestion," Sisko went on, turning back to the screen. "The Rylep ship will be allowed to dock and commence repairs, and the Aulep will be allowed to stay and do the same . . . for now. In the interim I will require both commanders to meet with me tonight. Is that clear?"

Dorram nodded.

Flenn, after a brief pause, did the same.

Sisko breathed a little sigh. "Good." The screen went instantly blank.

"The Rylep ship is maneuvering toward the station with thrusters," Worf reported.

"Very well," Sisko said. "Allow them to dock, but put a security detail on them."

"Yes, sir."

"Sisko out."

"Captain," Quark said, "will I be allowed to attend this meeting?"

"Oh, I insist!" Sisko bent over the Ferengi, leaving little distance between them. "Somehow, Quark, I'm certain you had a hand in getting us all into this mess. I'll be quite interested in hearing how you intend to get us out."

CHAPTER
6

SISKO COULD FEEL the tension in the air even before everyone was seated.

He already knew this was not going to be a pleasant meeting. The Aulep and Rylep commanders had readily agreed to join him at eighteen hundred hours in his office; the hard part had been persuading them to show up without a contingent of armed escorts. To allay their fears for their personal safety, Odo had stationed security personnel at their docking ports with the promise of full protection for everyone. Odo's men had escorted them to Sisko's office.

Since Aulep and Rylep had arrived, not one cordial word had been spoken. In fact, hardly anyone was speaking at all. They sat staring steadfastly at the pattern of stars so clearly visible through the large, eye-shaped portal just behind Sisko's desk.

"Is everyone comfortable?" Sisko asked, taking his seat, interrupting the two aliens' apparent concentration. Flenn and Dorram nodded, more or less; then each turned a cold, vexed glare on the other. Sisko was glad Odo had required two additional security officers to stay in the room. If ever a meeting seemed likely to break down into a fistfight, this was it. Odo himself stood between the visitors' chairs, back a pace, hands clasped behind him. Which was exactly where Sisko wanted him.

"This is a small office; you don't have stare so loudly," he said, trying to lighten the mood. He watched with slight amazement as the two leaders continued to glare at each other as if locked in silent mortal combat.

Seeing them like this, so close to each other, he found their similarities even more striking. The likeness extended from their physical features and mannerisms to their attitudes—and both struck him as particularly unpleasant.

"Good evening," Major Kira said in a lively tone, as the twin doors to Sisko's office hissed open. She glanced first at Sisko, then at Odo, and finally at the two visitors, who were staring at her, unblinking. She wore her usual uniform, its deep red and light salmon colors in stark contrast to the red-and-black or blue-and-black uniforms worn by Starfleet officers. The short series of ridges on the bridge of her nose made her gaze seem more intense, and the bounce of her short hair amplified the aura of energy she tended to emit. The Aulep and Rylep commanders seemed to find her enchanting.

The door opened again, and Quark entered, pausing directly behind Major Kira. He seemed more at ease than he had a few hours ago, but quick recoveries were among Quark's many talents, Sisko knew, so that was no surprise.

"I trust I haven't missed anything?" Quark said enthusiastically, then proceeded to greet everyone.

"No," Sisko said. "Things have been pretty quiet so far. Which leaves that first step up to me, I guess. So let's get started by making a couple of things clear. The Federation does not like being used, lied to, or fired upon, and neither do the Bajorans."

"And neither do we," Dorram said, "which is precisely what these Aulep *tlasatt* have done!"

Dorram had used a word for which the universal translator had no direct translation, but Sisko was fairly certain there were several human phrases that would have fit. Judging by the scowl on his face, Flenn seemed to understand it exactly.

"Your ship fired first," Sisko pointed out.

"And not only at the Aulep ship but on our station as well," Kira added.

"We have a right!" Dorram said. "The Aulep have wronged us and made you their accomplices, and they must be made to pay."

"What exactly have the Aulep done?" Sisko asked.

"Nothing, of course," Flenn said loudly. He sat back and folded his arms. "We are the victims here. Victims of an unprovoked attack by these ruthless—"

"You call *us* ruthless?" Dorram demanded.

"Yes, I do."

"And yet you find no crime against the Rylep beneath you!"

"I find the Rylep beneath me, that is for certain," Flenn said. He turned quickly to Sisko. "Captain, the Rylep are ruthless aggressors who will tell any lie, break any law, and attack any helpless world in order to expand their wealth and territories."

Sisko raised an eyebrow. "Is that so?"

"That in itself is a lie!" Dorram said, gripping the arms of his chair. "The Aulep are nothing more than ruthless pirates. They have preyed upon neighboring space lanes for years!"

Flenn looked less than amused.

"Well," Odo said, as Sisko looked at him, "at least they both agree on the 'ruthless' part."

Sisko in turn looked at Quark, who for the time being seemed inclined to say nothing at all. "I think we need to discuss a few particulars," Sisko told his visitors. "Don't you agree, Quark?"

"Oh, yes, I do," Quark said, glancing from person to person, all around the room, "but I have so few of them to discuss. Perhaps we could start with everyone else's particulars." He paused, then nodded benevolently at both the visitors.

"Very well, I will tell you of the Rylep's many crimes, Captain," Flenn offered. "I will tell you of the many races who fear the appearance of Rylep ships in their skies, of the helpless thousands they have exploited, even ruined, and then you can judge for yourself."

"And when you are through listening to this great fiction," Dorram said, his voice reduced to a growl not unlike that of a bullterrier, "I will tell you of the countless cargoes the Aulep have stolen, the crews who have died at their hands, the many worlds that live in fear of commercial ruin because Aulep pirates have cost them so dearly."

Flenn stood up and pointed a stubby orange finger at Dorram. "You would *dare* accuse us—"

"Indeed I would!" Dorram shouted, rising as well.

"I should have known better than to try meeting with you!" Flenn snarled back. "These station people should have blasted you from the skies the moment you appeared, just as I told them to!"

"If it wasn't for this station, you would not be alive to say such a thing!" Dorram said. "We would have blasted you from the stars!"

"Gentlemen, please!" Sisko pushed at the air in front of him with open palms, urging the two to settle down.

Flenn leaned across the table. "If I had a weapon—"

"Who needs one!" Dorram howled, and with that he lunged across the short distance between their chairs and wrapped both hands around the Aulep commander's neck.

Odo and his security team were on them in an instant, prying them apart. Sisko sighed. This was not going to be easy, he thought. At least Quark had managed to jump back against the wall, well out of harm's way.

"Lively pair, aren't they?" Odo said to Sisko as he tightened his grip on the struggling Rylep commander.

"I think this might have to wait until they've had a chance to calm down again," Kira said.

"I agree," Sisko said. "We aren't getting anywhere. Take them to back to their ships and keep them under guard."

Odo nodded. Then he and his men began shuffling Dorram and Flenn out the door.

"We'll meet again in three hours," Sisko called after his visitors. "And we'll keep on meeting until the two of you decide to settle down, tell me what I want to know, and work this out."

"From the looks of things, that might take a while," Quark said, apparently no more pleased with the results of the meeting than Sisko.

"Maybe," Sisko said. "But that is going to be up to them. And as for you, Quark," Sisko added, frowning, "I'm still convinced there's something you're not telling me. Either that, or you're a much bigger fool than most people take you for."

"There's no need for name-calling, Captain,"

Quark said snappishly. "And I hope you're happy. Perhaps you didn't notice, but I was trying to get a word in, and I got nothing for my trouble. Can I go now?"

"You're dismissed, but we'll see each other again in the morning," Sisko said.

Quark, summoning up as much indignation as he could manage, hurried out.

Sisko rose and trailed him out and down the short flight of steps to the main level in Ops. He glanced briefly about, noticing the half-dozen technicians manning the various stations, feeling a certain satisfaction at what he saw. Everything seemed to be running smoothly, for once.

"Mr. Worf," he said, as he looked toward Tactical. "I'll be in my quarters if anyone needs me."

"Yes, sir."

Sisko took the turbolift to the habitat ring, then strolled down the long, gently curving corridor to the suite he shared with his son. Inside, he found himself surrounded by the peace and quiet only one's personal quarters could provide. He didn't need that kind of break very often, but right now he was in a mood to afford himself the luxury. Possibly even a nap . . .

"I thought you'd never get back," Jake said, emerging from his room as Sisko paused before the replicator, contemplating a snack. He didn't feel up to cooking tonight.

Sisko fashioned a smile. "And why's that?"

"Well . . . you know."

"I do?"

"I'm ready for another runabout lesson."

Sisko saw the look of radiant excitement on Jake's face—the kind of look Sisko could never bring himself to crush, no matter how wretched he felt. He'd forgotten all about the lesson, of course. "When?"

"Now?" Jake asked, a bit sheepishly.

"I thought you'd say that."

Jake waited for a moment, then said, "And?"

It might not be a bad idea to get out of the station altogether for a while, Sisko thought. At least he could look at it that way. "Okay," he said. "Right now."

Sisko felt the tension start to lift as he strapped himself into his chair aboard the *Rio Grande*. No matter how long he spent in space, no matter how many missions he flew, there was always something exciting about lifting off and flying into the unknown. He saw that excitement mirrored in his son's eyes.

Fifteen minutes later, after they finished their systems checks, they released the docking clamps and lifted off from DS9 for a tour of the Bajoran system.

Jake's nervousness seemed to evaporate as he carefully executed each maneuver his father asked for, including a double turn at full impulse. An hour passed before Sisko let Jake spend a little time on the Ops consoles. Finally they turned and headed back to the station.

"I think you're really getting the hang of it," he told his son, brimming with honest pride.

"Yeah, well, I gotta impress my old man," Jake said.

The flight had been a short one, but it left Sisko feeling good, almost as good as Jake, who was grinning like a newly appointed starship captain on his maiden voyage.

Overall, Sisko thought, Jake's second lesson was a complete success, much as he had expected.

But tomorrow was another day. He had a second meeting with the Aulep and Rylep to look forward to, and he did not expect that to go nearly as well.

CHAPTER
7

"GOOD MORNING," SISKO said as his office doors slid apart to admit Flenn and Dorram, who were once again followed immediately by Odo and two security guards. Quark entered just behind them, looking every bit as sullen as the two commanders. They all stood about staring at one another.

"I said, good morning," Sisko repeated.

"There is nothing good about it," Dorram muttered.

"It's another expression," Sisko said. He indicated the chairs. "Please take your seats, try to relax, and we'll get started."

"My crew and I wish only to leave," Flenn said, "at once, and alone. We feel it reasonable to request that you detain the Rylep until we are safely away.

They are the ones, after all, who attacked your station and my ship without provocation."

"Without provocation?" Dorram responded instantly. "Are you listening to yourself? I swear, Flenn, we will hunt you down wherever you go!"

Flenn had his hands clasped together in his lap; he clenched them tighter now and raised his upper lip to expose small gray teeth. "Come ahead. We will be waiting."

Sisko glanced at Quark, who seemed to be sinking into an almost trancelike state. The Ferengi blinked, and Sisko noticed that the dark circles around his deep-set eyes seemed even darker than normal.

Quark cleared his throat. "This all sounds a bit hasty, don't you think? There must be some way we can work this out and keep from killing one another. Maybe we can even arrange a transaction that will be favorable to everyone. One that would speak to the future, perhaps. After all, there are many ways to slice a pie."

"A . . . pie?" Flenn asked.

Quark glanced at Sisko with an expression that made the captain think instantly of headache pain.

"You're doing fine, Quark," Sisko said.

"A pie—it's . . . another hu-man expression," Quark explained. "They've even got me doing it. What I mean is, there should be plenty of profits to go around. Let's take the proposed transaction between Flenn and me, for example. Perhaps we could divide payment between the two of you, or we could deal for one cargo now and more later on. That way, eventually everybody will be happy. I would even be willing to raise my offer—slightly, you understand—if it means we can all just get on with our lives."

Silence prevailed for several seconds. Then Flenn slowly turned to look at Dorram, took a breath, and said, "The Rylep would find a way to cheat us."

"The Aulep," Dorram countered, "would find a way to steal what is ours."

Flenn sat up, rigid. "You would lie!"

Dorram got to his feet. "You would attack!"

"You should talk!" Flenn snapped, also standing now. "This from the same commander who is guilty of the attempted murder of myself and my crew and the attempted destruction of an Aulep vessel in a neutral spacedock!"

"Have you forgotten that you are guilty of countless acts of economic sabotage!"

"Gentlemen, please, mistakes were made, of course, but the past need not determine the future," Quark said in a soothing voice.

The two captains continued to glare at each other. Dorram opened his mouth for another round of angry bickering.

Clearly, Sisko thought, Quark's words were having no effect on the pair. He gave a mental sigh. Time to intervene again.

Before Dorram could continue, Sisko rose and raised his deep voice to drown them out: "Perhaps one of you could explain the details to me, so I can understand how the two of you got to this point."

"That is simple, Captain," Dorram replied. "You cannot sell what you do not have. However, Flenn has an easy solution to that problem. He and his Aulep pirates steal whatever they want. Then they sell the booty as far away as possible, though they did not run far enough this time!"

"Is that so?" Odo said, looking at the Ferengi. "Fencing stolen goods, eh, Quark?"

Sisko frowned. "Stolen, you say? Did you know that, Quark? Exactly what sort of merchandise are we talking about?"

"Crystals!" Dorram declared.

The Ferengi glanced from one face to another. Sisko thought Quark looked genuinely shocked.

"Yes, it was a shipment of crystals," Quark said. He looked to Dorram. "But how did you know?"

"Because," Dorram shouted, "Flenn stole them from *me!*"

"*You* stole them, and you know it!" Flenn shouted back. "So you had no legal claim. We had just as much right to the crystals as you did."

"But *we* stole them *first!*" Dorram screamed, pounding his fists on the arms of his chair.

Sisko glared at Quark, whose whole face had darkened noticeably. He began to squirm in his seat. "I swear," he said, his voice sounding suddenly a little hoarse, "I didn't know *any* of this."

"Stealing from a thief doesn't count, does it, Captain?" Flenn asked, quite serious.

"And who can believe him, Captain?" Dorram said.

Sisko balked. It seemed they had suddenly decided to appoint him arbiter. And now he wasn't sure he wanted the job. He would have been just as happy to have them both off the station and out of his life.

He took a breath. "It sounds like neither one of you has a claim to the crystals."

"Gentlemen, once again, please!" Quark said, interrupting, "I can still help in many ways, I assure you. And I see no reason why we can't start right now to work out a reasonable, equitable deal between—"

"I don't see how any of these arguments matter," Flenn said, seeming a little less angry but obviously quite disgusted. "Not after Dorram and his blast-happy Rylep crew decided to start shooting indiscriminately." Flenn looked at Dorram again. "That cargo on my ship was irreplaceable, and you destroyed it! Only a fool would have taken such a chance, as you have clearly demonstrated. Now neither of us can—"

"Excuse me!" Quark said, stepping directly between the two opponents. "Did you say—did you say *destroyed?*"

"When they attacked," Flenn said, nodding.

"He is telling the truth—this time," Dorram said.

Quark's gaze darted from Aulep to Rylep to Sisko and back. "You—" he squeaked. Then he tried again, "You mean that debris I saw floating away in space just after the attack, that was my . . . my crystals?"

Both aliens nodded.

Quark stepped back on wobbly legs. His eyes went wide and fixed, and his jaw went slack. He groped the air, found the arm of his chair, and lowered himself clumsily into it.

"Are you all right, Quark?" Sisko asked.

Quark made a small, weak sound somewhere in the back of his throat.

Odo turned to Sisko and folded his arms. "I would guess," he said, "that was a no."

Elliena gazed out through the *Rio Grande*'s main viewport from the seat next to Jake, hands folded in her lap. She hadn't said a word since coming aboard. Jake didn't know if something was wrong, if he'd done something to offend her.

They hadn't seen each other in more than three weeks, yet after their initial greetings and small talk, the mood had changed to one of quiet assessment. It made him uneasy. He found himself increasingly eager to say something and move on; he just didn't know what.

Finally he tapped at several of the panels in front of him, checking secondary systems. He wanted to get under way. But there was little he could do to speed things up. He didn't dare power the runabout up. Not yet. You didn't gain big privileges by messing up on the little ones.

He took a breath. "It shouldn't be much longer," he said, finally breaking their silence. "Chief

O'Brien said he'd be here as soon as he finished with—"

Jake paused. Elliena had very little technical expertise. She was a student of the arts, which was one of the things that had drawn him to her. O'Brien was busy running a diagnostic on the station transporter's replacement phase transition coils—which wouldn't mean a thing to Elliena. He didn't want to bury her in technobabble.

"When he's finished with some maintenance checks," he said instead.

"That's all right," Elliena said in a voice that reminded Jake of a young Kira Nerys, a comparison made even easier by Elliena's appearance. She was slightly shorter than the major, and her complexion was perhaps a bit darker, but her petite, intelligent face and measured manner were similar—except for Elliena's smile, which was entirely her own. She wore her hair slightly long and curled under and forward at the neck, still a popular style on Bajor, and her ankle-length dress covered with subtle brown-on-tan scrollwork patterns, was quite Bajoran as well. She said that her parents insisted on formality both in clothing and in manners, but Jake suspected she enjoyed it.

"I've only met Chief O'Brien once. Is he as good an engineer as I've heard?"

"Actually," Jake said, "he's better."

Elliena smiled. "Oh."

They sat quietly once again. Jake ran through a

thousand things to say to her in his head, but somehow they all sounded stupid. The last thing he wanted was to embarrass himself in front of her.

"It was nice of Chief O'Brien to offer to take us out," Elliena finally said.

"Yeah, the chief's a great guy. My dad asked him to help with my flight training, and he said he would."

"And he doesn't mind having me along?"

"No. I asked."

"Good."

Jake took a breath, let it out. They sat again for a while. Finally he decided to try a new tack.

"To tell you the truth, I hope their Bajor resources survey isn't going very well," he said, waiting for her reaction and guessing she would understand.

"Oh, me too," she said, just as he'd hoped.

Jake caught himself grinning a little too much, but Elliena quickly joined in.

"You know, with any luck, they'll be at it for months," she added. Which of course meant Elliena would be visiting for months as well. She looked about to giggle.

Jake let his grin disappear as a splash of reality entered his mind. He knew that his father and Elliena's parents, along with the technicians who were working on the project, were much too talented to allow the project to drag on so long. It was scheduled to run for another three months at the outside. But if experience was any indicator, it would probably conclude early.

"Something wrong?" Elliena asked.

"No, not exactly," he said, banishing his pessimistic thoughts. They had this time together; why spoil it by thinking too far into the future? "Besides, right now I'm doing everything I can to make things right. I'm spending time with you, and I'm working on upgrading my pilot status."

"Maybe we'll get to spend a little time alone together before I have to go back to Bajor," Elliena said, looking at him with what had to be her most polite smile. Their relationship hadn't taken any sharp romantic turns yet, but Jake had begun to suspect there was a strong possibility it might. He hoped this was a clear sign that Elliena felt the same way.

"Maybe," Jake replied. They stared into each other's eyes. He wasn't sure her parents would approve of their relationship if it did get serious, but he was increasingly certain that he did. Jake was acutely aware, as he sat gazing at her now, that for the moment at least they were completely alone. He wasn't sure of what do next. Did she want him to get up and put his arms around her right this minute? Did she want him to ask?

"O'Brien to the *Rio Grande.*" The chief's Irish lilt rang crisp and clear from the runabout's comm speaker, interrupting Jake's train of though

"Jake Sisko here, Chief," he said.

"Sorry, Jake, but I've been detained. We had some minor power fluctuations in the main energizing coils. I think we've got it smoothed out, but I want to run another simulation to make sure. It shouldn't take too long. Ten minutes at the most."

"Okay, Chief. We aren't going anywhere."

"See that you don't," the chief barked, though Jake could picture his grin as he spoke. A tone signaled O'Brien's sign-off.

"I may be going back to Bajor again sooner than I thought," Elliena told him. "For a couple of weeks or more this time. My parents have to analyze some of the new resource data before they can continue. I guess there are some funding questions involved."

"Maybe they'll let you stay here on the station," Jake suggested, something he was sure she had been thinking as well, even though she hadn't mentioned it.

"I've already suggested the idea," she replied, "but they didn't seem too thrilled. They let me stay here last night while they went down to Bajor to attend a meeting, but that was only because they're returning this morning. The next time they leave, I'll have to go with them." She slowly let out a sigh.

"I . . . I see," Jake said. That wasn't what he wanted at all, but he wasn't sure what to do about it, if anything.

"A few months ago it might have been different," she went on. "But with all the trouble lately, they're concerned about my safety—and theirs. That's why they've been so reluctant to move to *Deep Space Nine* even temporarily." She laughed. "They're not *completely* paranoid, but almost. They can't help worrying, at least in the backs of their minds, about the threat of an invasion by the Dominion, about the Klingons going to war with the Federation, and about the Cardassians changing their government again and coming back—not to mention all the ordinary disasters that can happen in space. They've got all the statistics."

"I understand," Jake said. "And I guess I'd feel the same if it was my daughter who wanted to stay."

This seemed to please Elliena in no small way. "I bet your father never worries about you," she said, eyes wide, a smile just beginning. She was watching him closely.

Jake thought his answer over carefully. "Not as much as he used to," he said. Elliena's smile grew a little wider.

"Look," Jake said, as a minor change in one of the runabout's Ops panel displays caught his eye. He keyed the main viewer and began scanning near space. The image showed Bajor in the distance, as well as countless stars. A planetary shuttle was leaving a low orbit around Bajor, silently, gracefully taking up a trajectory that would bring it to a rendezvous with DS9. Jake found Elliena watching the view as well. It was different from the one they could see through the runabout's two large front windows—that of the station's towering upper docking pylons.

On the screen they watched the shuttle's engines glow briefly, adjusting its course as it began to grow larger.

"That's the only space travel I've ever known,"

Elliena said, an edge of excitement in her voice. "Here and back."

"You're really looking forward to this flight, aren't you?" Jake said.

Elliena grinned. "It will be an adventure."

Jake grinned back. "Definitely." He checked the time impatiently; O'Brien would be along any minute, which would not be soon enough.

Flenn and Dorram were on their feet again.

"You would see us cut off from the universe if you had your way!" the Aulep commander shouted, waving his arms wildly.

"Cut you off? We should do the universe a favor instead and cut you in half!" Dorram thundered.

"That's all I'd expect you to say!"

"Is it?" Dorram said. "Admit that you and your thieving crew have attempted to—"

"While you and your murderous crew—"

"Gentlemen, I don't see this argument getting us anywhere," Sisko interrupted yet again. He had been trying without success to make them see the sense of polite discussion and compromise, and he was getting tired of it. He looked to Quark, but the Ferengi remained silent and absolutely motionless in his chair, staring straight ahead. He hadn't moved an inch since learning his crystals had been destroyed.

"Captain," Flenn said, "why don't you simply tell these Rylep that they are not welcome here and send them away?"

"Perhaps it is the Aulep who are not welcome,"

Dorram quickly countered. "You have no cargo to sell, so you have no business here, and you certainly aren't making any friends."

"We have no cargo because of you!" Flenn snapped, stepping forward and balling his stubby fingers into a fist. Odo held him back while one of the security guards took a step closer to Dorram.

"What I'd like to know," Sisko said, no longer in a conciliatory mood, "is who those crystals were stolen from to begin with."

The two visiting commanders said nothing. After a pause, Sisko looked the question to Quark, who had apparently returned to the here and now. The Ferengi rolled his eyes.

"I know that sickly look of yours, Quark."

"What look?" Quark said, holding his hands up and nervously bouncing stiff fingers off one another.

Sisko leaned across his desk. "You know exactly what I mean. And I'd say you know exactly whose crystals they were. If you're withholding that information—"

"No, Captain," Quark interrupted, swallowing as his voice cracked. "But you're right, I am sick. I need to lie down for a while."

Sisko dropped any pretense of patience. "Listen to me, Quark. If you know anything, you had better spit it out right now."

"Come on, Quark," Odo said in a gravelly voice, "Answer the nice captain."

"Honestly," Quark said, "I don't know where the crystals came from. But I do know who the *buyer* was to be. And that's what concerns me. He's not going to be happy."

Odo said, "Somehow I don't feel very sorry for you."

Sisko leaned toward Quark, all ears. "And who would this buyer be?"

The intercom sounded, followed by Commander Worf's resonant voice: "Ops to Captain Sisko."

"What is it?" Sisko said. He hoped it wasn't another emergency.

"A ship is emerging from the wormhole," Worf said. "They do not answer our hails. We are attempting to identify them."

"Is it a Jem'Hadar ship?"

"I do not believe so, sir."

"Very well," Sisko said, taking a deep breath. "I'll be right there. Sisko out."

Rising, he nodded to Odo. "See what else you can find out." He headed for the door.

"With pleasure," Odo said, smiling.

CHAPTER
8

"WHAT'S OUR STATUS?" Sisko asked as he jogged down the steps from his office to the floor of Ops. All eyes glanced up at him, then immediately went back to their duty stations.

"Captain, I have identified the ship," Worf reported. "It is Klingon. A military-class freighter."

"We've been trying to make contact," Dax said. "They're accelerating straight toward the station."

"Prepare to raise shields," Sisko told Worf. "Dax, put them on-screen."

On the main viewer Sisko watched a small dot appear against the backdrop of the wormhole, whose swirling, receding rings of brilliant blue and white were still visible from the ship's passage through it. In a blink, the wormhole seemed to vanish again.

"Magnify," Sisko said. The dot became a long,

dark spacecraft, narrow toward the front, bulky in the middle, a wide wedge configuration at the stern. Hard angles in dark gray characterized its hull. Even at a glance, Sisko could tell it was of Klingon design.

"Captain," Worf said clearly and unaffectedly, "sensors indicate the freighter's warp core is on the verge of overload. The entire vessel has sustained heavy damage. That may explain why they are not responding to your hail. I am reading enough life signs to account for most of the crew."

Sisko eyed the screen. "What kind of damage have they sustained, Mr. Worf?"

"Residual energy patterns indicate heavy weapons fire. Captain," Worf added, looking up from his consoles as Sisko turned to him, "that freighter is well armed, and its crew would normally include a number of trained Klingon warriors."

"Is it possible the Jem'Hadar attacked them?" Sisko asked as Major Kira entered Ops from the turbolift and went straight to her station.

"The Klingons would have fought back," Dax remarked.

"Strike patterns do not match those typical of Jem'Hadar weapons," Worf continued. "They are—" He paused, touching pads on his console, apparently rechecking his data. He looked up once more, mild consternation on his face.

"What is it?" Sisko asked.

"Sir, the burns appear to match those made by Klingon disrupters."

"So it's possible the Klingons are fighting each

other," Sisko considered out loud. It had happened before . . . but in the Gamma Quadrant?

"Possible but unlikely," Dax said. "Other weapons would leave similar traces. I'd say somebody surprised them."

"But who would attack the Klingons?" Kira asked. "It isn't like Klingons to run from a fight, so we have to assume that whoever attacked them either retreated or was destroyed."

"We don't know that they're running from anything," Sisko said. "But you're right. Klingons don't usually retreat."

"Captain," Worf said, "I'm getting a message from the freighter. Audio only."

Sisko's brow went up. *Good.* "Put it on."

"This is . . . Captain Dolras of . . . Klingon freighter *Toknor,* on—"

Static filled the air, replacing the Klingon's halting, shaken voice. Sisko straightened in response. Either this Dolras was a most atypical Klingon or he had been through a pretty bad time.

"Can you get them back?" he asked Dax.

"Give me a moment," Dax replied, working at her controls. The static began to subside, and then the voice returned, faint but understandable.

"We require immediate assistance," Dolras said. "You and your station are about to come under attack."

Sisko looked at his officers, who seemed as surprised as he was. "I see," Sisko said. "We can arrange docking space for you, and we can have a medical team standing by to help with any wounded, but I'd like to know what you mean by an attack. From whom?"

"I wish I could tell you, Captain," Dolras said, fading again. "But the threat they bring should be your greatest concern. Look what they have done to—"

The voice was gone in a wash of noise.

"Please repeat. Your signal is garbled," Sisko said with some urgency.

". . . must prepare defenses . . . immediately!" Dolras said, this last coming across clear enough.

Sisko still couldn't see any other ship, and he wasn't getting any reports of sightings from his crew. "Who attacked you?" he asked. Again, static came back. He turned to Dax once more.

"We've lost him again, Captain," she reported. "I don't know if I'll be able to—"

"Captain," Worf interrupted, looking up from his console. "Another contact, coming through the wormhole."

Sisko snapped his head around. He could see the colorful swirl of the wormhole forming again behind the Klingon freighter. The *Toknor* had slowed, approaching the station. The damage to its hull was clearly visible, and it was extensive.

"Identification?" Sisko asked, keeping his eyes on the screen as a second vessel appeared. Dolras hadn't been able to give them much time to prepare.

"It is another Klingon freighter, identical to the first," Worf replied.

"They are following the flight path of the *Toknor* exactly," Kira said.

"Hail them," Sisko told Dax. "Maybe they can shed a little more light on all of this."

"Captain," Worf said, "I recommend we arm all weapons. If these freighters are part of a Klingon military convoy, whoever attacked them might have followed them here, just as Dolras warned. Perhaps—" He cut himself off, eyes darting down to the displays at his fingertips. "The second freighter has opened fire."

Sisko watched a luminous energy pulse emanate from the second freighter and strike at Dolras's ship. The bright bloom of a starboard-side explosion gave testimony to the attacker's accuracy.

"That answers a few questions," Kira said coldly.

In three quick steps Sisko made his way to the large central Ops console, just opposite Kira's position. "Captain Dolras," he said, tapping at the lighted panel beneath his fingers, "bring your ship around to these coordinates. That should put the station between you and the other freighter. Meanwhile, can you tell us anything about your situation? Why are your own people firing on you?"

"Captain," Kira said, "I'm not sure Dolras can maneuver well enough to get behind us."

"The second freighter has fired again, Captain," Worf stated, confirming what Sisko was seeing. "Another direct hit. The *Toknor* has no shields remaining. Warp and impulse engines are completely off-line."

"Captain, the *Toknor*'s hull has been breached," Kira said. "They're losing atmospheric integrity."

Again Sisko watched the screen intently. The *Toknor* had begun to drift to port as a visible cloud of gas, crystallizing as it encountered the cold of space, formed on its starboard side. His eyes widened as a long section of the hull tumbled free, beginning a random journey toward the outer reaches of the Bajoran solar system.

"I'm still reading life signs; they're not all dead," Kira said. "And I'm picking up thruster discharge. Dolras must be trying to regain control."

"No," Worf said flatly. "As far as I can determine, their forward disrupter banks are still functional and partially charged."

"So they're still trying to fight back," Sisko said, letting his voice trail off as the idea settled in his mind. That, he thought, sounded like the Klingons he was used to.

"The *Toknor* is firing," Worf said.

Sisko witnessed the disrupter discharge. Their aim was accurate, but the pulse seemed to pass right through the attacking vessel. There was no visible damage to the second ship. Sisko stared in disbelief. What he was seeing was simply impossible.

"Captain," Worf said, "I am unable to get a lock on the second freighter. It is as if it isn't there."

"They still won't answer our hails," Dax said.

"Arm weaponry," Sisko commanded, which drew a satisfied nod from Worf. The *Toknor* was close enough now to be fully visible. Sisko flinched involuntarily at what he saw. It was clear that the damaged freighter would not be able to drag itself around to the far side of the station, out of harm's way. The station's shields would have to be lowered to allow the vessel to come straight in and dock, but Sisko couldn't risk doing that just now; there was no telling what the second freighter might do, given the chance. He couldn't beam the *Toknor*'s crew off, either. The same dangers applied.

"Major Kira, how close is the *Toknor*?" he asked. "Can we get a tractor beam on the ship and tow it in close enough to extend our shields around it?"

"They are within range," Kira answered.

Sisko nodded. "Good. Do it."

"Tractor beam locked," Kira replied. "It's working. Preparing to extend shields."

"The second freighter is returning fire," Worf reported.

"Direct hit," Dax said an instant later.

"They're firing again," Worf said.

Sisko looked up in time to see the second energy burst strike Dolras's vessel amidships. He was forced to shield his eyes against the blinding explosion that followed, filling the screen and all of near space with its white-hot fury. A shock wave followed straight on the heels of the flash and struck the station with a sudden forceful punch that sent Sisko tumbling across the deck. The station's lights dimmed as the floor pitched, then shuddered badly, rattling teeth and bones, but the sudden darkness was quickly lit once more as overloaded plasma conduits spewed energy from half a dozen Ops consoles. Slowly the floor moved back to level, and the emergency lighting kicked in. Sisko scrambled to his feet. "Is everyone all right?"

He got nods from the bridge crew; most of them had managed to cling to their stations. Sisko found one exception quickly enough: Ensign Ballard, one of his newest Ops officers, lay on the floor, unconscious, burn marks on her hands and uniform.

"Sisko to Bashir, we need a medical team up here right away!" He turned to his officers. "What the hell just happened?"

"The blast occurred just as I was attempting to reconfigure the shields around the freighter," Kira said. "Most of the force was directed inward, toward the station. We lost the shields for a moment, but I've got them back."

"Damage reports are coming in from all over the station," Dax said. "Some of it appears to be heavy. I'm trying to determine how serious our casualties are."

"The *Toknor* has been completely destroyed," Worf answered, his voice showing none of the emotion Sisko knew he must be feeling. On the main viewscreen only a spreading cloud of debris could been seen where Dolras's ship had been a moment ago.

"Hail that freighter till you get an answer!" Sisko said, glaring at the screen. "And try to open a channel to the Klingon sector command. Anybody you can get."

"Sir," Worf said, followed by a rumble from somewhere deep in his throat as he stood shaking his head at his consoles. He took a breath. "I've been running a full sensor sweep on the remaining freighter." He paused again, fingers moving, making the console beep and chime.

"What is it, Mr. Worf?" Sisko prodded.

"It's as if there is nothing there. I can detect no life signs and no drive signature of any type."

"You mean . . . any *known* type," Sisko suggested.

"No, sir. I mean there is no evidence of any kind of propulsion system, no active hull echoes, no life-support system or shield energy. I am picking up trace energy readings, but nothing else. It is possible our weapons would be useless against the target, just as the *Toknor*'s were."

"Can we use a tractor beam on it?"

Worf shook his head, and Sisko saw a mix of frustration and disappointment on the Klingon's features. "I do not think so."

"Captain," Dax said, "I'm receiving distress calls from several ships in dock. At least one of them has been blown clear of its moorings. And I've got another message coming in from a Bajoran planetary shuttle that was on approach. They were caught in the blast and are going to require assistance."

"Very well, get crews to the runabouts and launch them right away. In the meantime—"

"Benjamin!"

Dax's tone caught Sisko's immediate attention. He looked at her, watched her stricken expression as she paid keen attention to another message.

"What is it, Dax?" he asked, taking a step toward her.

"The *Rio Grande* is drifting free. It must have been caught in the blast wave like the others." Dax's eyes came to his. "Benjamin, Chief O'Brien was going to take Jake and Elliena out today. They may be in the runabout."

Sisko nodded gravely, recalling the fact, feeling his stomach harden. "Is the chief with them now?"

Dax tapped the comm. "Ops to Chief O'Brien."

The chime rang back almost at once. "O'Brien here. I'm on my way to Ops. I'll be there in a few seconds."

"Where are Jake and Elliena?" Sisko asked.

"They're aboard a runabout," O'Brien replied.

Sisko looked at the main viewer. "They're alone," he said, scanning the image on the screen. "Try to raise them."

"I've got Jake on the comm," Dax said after a pause. "I'll put him on."

Sisko held a deep breath, then let it out as the faces of Jake and Elliena appeared on the screen, taking the place of the stars and the second Klingon freighter. "Are the two of you all right?"

"Yes, I think so," Jake replied, sounding a bit short of breath but otherwise calm.

"We got bounced around a little," Elliena said.

She was clearly shaken, but appeared to be holding her own.

"I bet you did," Sisko said. "Jake, what's your status?"

"The runabout has been damaged, but I'm not sure how bad it is. I can try to get an idea."

"I'm not reading any systems failures," Kira reported. "But main power wasn't online to begin with."

"If they can get the runabout powered up," Sisko said, "will Jake be able to navigate?"

Kira shrugged. "I don't see why not."

"What about using our tractor beam on the *Rio Grande?*"

"We should be able to latch on," Kira said.

"Captain," Worf said, "doing so would draw attention to the runabout, and it was just after our beam was activated that the *Toknor* was destroyed. The two may have no connection, but the second freighter is still at point-blank range. If they should open fire . . ."

"I see your point," Sisko said, "but for the moment they don't seem to be doing anything at all."

Worf checked his console. "Confirmed."

The captain raised his voice to the intercom once more. "Jake, listen to me. We can't beam you off without dropping the shields, but the runabout seems functional. I want you to get the engines online, then raise the runabout's shields. After that, take the helm, but wait for my instructions. We're going to try to pull you in, but if anything goes wrong, you may have to fly the *Rio Grande* yourself."

"Yes, sir," Jake said evenly, though Sisko could see a look of tense excitement on his son's face, which was exactly what he would have expected.

"Are my parents on the station?" Elliena asked, sounding nervous but steady.

"I don't have that information," Sisko told her. "As I recall, they were due back today. I'll have someone look into it at once. We'll tell them what's going on."

"Thank you, Captain," Elliena said.

Sisko turned briefly, letting his gaze find each of his Ops officers. "All right, let's make sure we can give them a happy ending."

Everyone went to work. Sisko made his way up to Worf's tactical station, where he carefully watched as the sensors indicated the precise rise of power levels aboard the *Rio Grande.* When the runabout's shields were activated at full power, Sisko gave the signal. A wide, oscillating tractor beam reached out into space and touched its target, illuminating the *Rio Grande,* turning it slightly as it was set in motion.

"The runabout has been engaged," Dax reported. "We're pulling them in."

The screen went back to the original external view. Then Sisko's eyes went wide as he witnessed a second beam, very much like the one from the station, suddenly appear and touch the runabout from a different direction.

"Captain," Worf snapped, "the Klingon freighter has activated a tractor beam."

"They're attempting to pull the runabout toward them," Kira said, anxiously tapping at her panel.

"Go to maximum power!" Sisko barked.

"Already there, Captain," Kira responded. "The freighter is matching us exactly. . . . Wait!" Kira bit her lip as she stared intently at her displays. "They're increasing power. We're losing the runabout."

Sisko slammed his fist on the console before him. "Suggestions!"

"Sir," Worf said, "at full thrust the *Rio Grande*'s engines, combined with our tractor beam, may provide enough power to overcome the pull of the other beam."

Sisko stood for an instant considering the probabilities. "It might work."

"I believe it is their only chance," Worf attested.

"Jake," Sisko said, "can you hear me?"

"Yes," Jake said. His voice quavered, and Sisko realized the runabout must be shaking itself apart. "What's going on?"

"I think this ship is going to break up any second now. I've lost control. I don't think——"

"I know, Jake. Can you verify that you have the engines online?"

"Yes, but the helm isn't responding."

"That's because that freighter is trying to pull you away from the station. We can't fight it alone, so you're going to have to help us get you free." He turned to Kira. "Major, give him a heading for maximum combined effect, away from the freighter but not too close to the station—we don't want him to crash into us if this works. Jake, enter the heading, and when I tell you to, go to full impulse. Give it everything you've got."

"Confirmed," Jake answered, breathless. "Course laid in."

Sisko waited only a moment. "Okay, Jake, full thrust!"

"Firing engines—now," Jake said.

"They're coming around," Kira said.

Sisko stood staring at the viewer, focusing all his attention on the small dark spot that was the *Rio Grande* caught in the crisscrossed tractor beams. He could see the glow from the runabout's engines and could estimate the amount of combined energy that was being spent on that one place in space right now, the place that held his only son and a Bajoran diplomat's only daughter.

"The freighter is still increasing power to its tractor beam," Kira said. "I don't know where they're getting it from, but I don't think it'll be enough to hold the *Rio Grande.*"

Dax shook her head. "The runabout's engines are beginning to overload. If this doesn't work in the next few seconds Jake is going to have to shut down."

"Mr. Worf, how are we doing?" Sisko asked.

"The runabout is beginning to shear away," the commander replied, eyes fixed on his console.

"They might just do it," Kira agreed.

"They are free!" Worf shouted. with enough excitement to cause Sisko to look at him with surprise.

On the screen the small dark spot they had been observing suddenly darted away from the intersecting tractor beams. Sisko continued to watch, jubilant at first, then going cold as he realized the runabout was spinning out of control.

"Jake, shut down the engines!" he shouted. "Use your thrusters. You have to regain helm control."

"I'm—I'm trying," Jake replied shakily.

"He doesn't have the experience to deal with anything like this," Sisko said, thinking out loud. He gripped the console so hard that his hands began to hurt.

"Captain," Kira reported, looking up at Sisko. "They're headed straight for the wormhole."

As she spoke, the vast bright whirlpool of swirling circles that signified the opening of the wormhole erupted on the screen. The *Rio Grande* spun toward its open mouth, out of reach, out of control, falling into the spiral's central fury, then vanishing from sight.

Sisko stood by, stunned, holding a breath, unable to let it out. The wormhole disappeared again, leaving only the empty darkness of space.

"The second freighter is moving off," Worf said, proving himself the only officer whose attention was not entirely focused on the runabout. "But . . . this is not possible," Worf said.

Sisko slowly turned to his strategic operations

officer, slightly numb. "What is not possible, Mr. Worf?"

"It is . . . that is . . ." He stopped, apparently collecting his thoughts. "The entire vessel seems to be fading from sight."

"Magnify," Sisko said. The Klingon freighter suddenly filled the main viewer. But where definitive detail should have been visible, he saw stars beginning to show through the ship's ponderous hull.

"The ship is moving into the wormhole," Worf added as the wormhole appeared once more immediately ahead of the freighter's advancing bow.

Following Jake! Sisko thought, as he watched the freighter grow more faint, like a ghostly mirage, fading into the wormhole, until it vanished altogether from sight.

CHAPTER
9

CHIEF MILES O'BRIEN shook his head in frustration. He'd been going over the events involving the two Klingon freighters, working with the Ops personnel who had been there. A lot of the data didn't make any sense, but admitting that wasn't getting him anywhere. He'd been an engineer for too many years to be left scratching his head, especially with an impatient captain looking over his shoulder. He stood back from the central Ops station and used the back of his hand to wipe the dampness from his forehead, then put both palms flat on either side of the console displays as if willing them to cooperate.

"I'm afraid none of us has many answers," Sisko said. "We'll just have to keep at it until we get some."

"Well, sir," O'Brien said, running his fingers through his short locks, "I do have quite a few questions. That first freighter was real enough; the debris is still floating around out there. And the readings in the sensor logs leave no doubt that the disrupters the second freighter used were real enough as well—and Klingon, I'd say; the readings are almost textbook."

"Almost?" Sisko asked.

O'Brien nodded. "Yes, but not quite. Disrupters bleed plasma all over the place when they're fired. They leave a trail of polarized energy wherever they go. In a system like this, the solar wind dissipates the trail eventually, but that can take weeks. I've got clear trails from the disrupters fired by the *Toknor,* but almost nothing from those fired by the other ship."

"But the second freighter was identical to the first," Worf noted, "and definitely Klingon."

"They both *seemed* authentic enough," Kira said, "except that one of them vanished without a trace."

"If they were using a cloaking device, it's not like any I've ever seen," Sisko added.

"That class of ship is not ordinarily equipped with cloaking equipment," Worf said. "But even if that one was, the captain is right. No known cloaking device would explain what we saw."

"When the second freighter was visible, we should have gotten normal readings," Dax said, barely looking up from her continuing scans. "But throughout the encounter, our sensors detected almost nothing."

"Agreed," Sisko said. "And both Klingon and Romulan technology becomes fully effective within seconds after it is activated. That second freighter disappeared a little bit at a time, almost as if it had never been there at all."

"As if it was being sucked into the wormhole a particle at a time," Kira said, setting the chief's imagination in motion.

"Those are both good possibilities," O'Brien told her. "I mean, according to the logs, when that second ship was here, it was hardly here at all. It was like some kind of particle projection or hologram."

"I doubt anyone on the receiving end of that freighter's weapons fire would agree with that assessment," Sisko said. "Including Jake, Elliena, and the crew of the *Toknor*."

O'Brien nodded, finding himself for the most part back where he'd started. Clearly some unknown technology was at work.

"Chief," Dax said, clearly concentrating as she worked at her station, "I may have something here. A ship's engines leave a trail, too. I just ran a sweep, and I'm picking up a pattern of charged neutrino particles. It's faint and spreading, but I'm sure they were left by one of those two Klingon freighters." She looked up. "I'd say the first one. They lead straight back through the wormhole."

"Which means they might lead to a matching stream on the other side," O'Brien suggested.

"And maybe to wherever those Klingon ships came from," Kira said, "and what it was they were fighting over."

Dax nodded, adding a slight grin.

"At least that gives us a direction to look in," Sisko said. "I have to admit I don't like any of the possibilities. For all we know, the Klingons might be trying to trade with the Dominion, or they may be developing a new weapons system. We could be walking into a lot of trouble."

"Both are . . . unlikely," Worf said. "But an investigation would seem to be in order."

Sisko nodded. "How long has it been since the wormhole closed?" he asked Dax.

She glanced down. "If Jake was able to return, he should have been back by now."

"I'd say you're right," Sisko replied.

"Are you going after them yourself, sir?" the chief asked, already certain that Sisko would go; that was what O'Brien would have done if his daughter, Molly, had been aboard the *Rio Grande*.

"Yes, but first I need all the information I can get," Sisko replied. "Jake and Elliena aren't the only ones I'm responsible for. We have to assume that the second freighter somehow went back through the wormhole, if it was ever completely in this quadrant in the first place."

"You mean something like the holographic projection idea," Dax said.

Sisko kept his sigh to himself. "I don't know what I mean. Chief O'Brien is right. We've got disappearing ghost ships, Klingon against Klingon, unprovoked attacks on a Federation runabout, and for now we can't even begin to figure out what the hell is going on."

He paused to consider everyone in Ops for a moment, then settled again on Kira. "Major, have there been any reports or rumors of problems, anomalies, anything unusual in the Gamma Quadrant?"

"None that I know of," she said.

Sisko looked around him. "Has anyone else heard anything that might be significant?"

"No," Worf said, mildly apologetic. "I have not."

"Me either," O'Brien said, feeling the same way. "Even the Jem'Hadar have been quiet lately," he added, trying to sound at least somewhat helpful.

"There were two routine navigational reports from a Ferengi trade ship, just this past week," Kira said, tapping at her console. She waited a moment, sucking lightly at her lower lip, then abruptly nodded. "Here it is." She paused again, then frowned. "It isn't anything, really. Both reports describe a dark body, mass and configuration appropriate to a large moon or planetoid. It was seen drifting through the nearest part of the Myalon Corridor, just a few light-years from the other side of the wormhole. But if you're looking for something worth arguing over, there aren't many other candidates."

"The Myalon Corridor?" O'Brien asked. He'd heard it mentioned a couple of times before, but didn't know what it was, exactly.

Dax said, "It's an extended area containing relatively few stars. We understand it's a commonly traveled space lane in that sector, especially for anyone wishing to avoid passing through Dominion territories."

"Doesn't sound too promising. I mean, there are lots of stray planetoids around," O'Brien remarked.

"Agreed," Sisko said. "What else?"

No one said a word.

"Very well," the captain told them, "we'll just have to make something turn up. I'm not going to wait any longer. Transfer all available data on those freighters and those navigation reports to one of the runabouts. Major, I'm leaving you in command." Sisko glanced up at Worf, who outranked Major Kira, but the Klingon did not question the order.

"Wouldn't you rather take the *Defiant*?" Kira asked.

"We've been doing a little maintenance on her," O'Brien told her. "It'll take a couple of hours to get the engines back online."

"I don't want to wait that long," Sisko said.

"I'll have the *Rubicon* ready in just a few minutes," O'Brien said. He stepped over to one of the consoles and began transferring composite sensor data. Finishing, he started toward the turbolift, then paused before stepping on. "Coming, Captain?"

"We have plenty of people who can see to the runabout, Chief."

"I know, sir, but I'd like to go along. You'll need

someone with you. And if the *Rio Grande* is damaged, you'll need an engineer."

"I see. Any other reasons?" Sisko asked, letting a decidedly congenial expression start to show as he joined the chief.

"Yes, sir, I guess there are. I'd like to know how a Klingon freighter with no mass and no drive could do what that one did, then just disappear."

That wasn't all, and O'Brien had already guessed that Sisko knew it. He and Jake had been friends for some time.

"And?" the captain prodded.

"I feel a little responsible for what's happened to Jake and Elliena," O'Brien admitted.

"I don't understand why. It's not your fault. No one could have predicted that Klingon attack."

"I know, but if I'd been there, I might have been able to get them back. Either way, I guess I'm just worried about that kid of yours."

"Very well," he told O'Brien, extending his hand. "Welcome aboard."

Major Kira felt a twinge of trepidation as she watched the runabout status displays, double-checking as Sisko and O'Brien put the *Rubicon* through a brief systems check, then powered it up for departure. Kira had her work cut out for her today. Dax was already smoothing ruffled feathers, since the comm channels were filled with panicked civilians trying to find out what had happened and how soon they could leave DS9. Dozens of ships had been damaged while docked at the station, and then there was the crippled Bajoran shuttle, which had managed to creep within range of DS9's tractor beam and was only now being brought gently in. Besides DS9's guests, many of the station's residents, both permanent and temporary, could be less than accommodating. Every bruise and bump, once Doctor Bashir finished treating them, was sure to find voice before the day was out.

The major still hadn't gotten full damage reports on the station itself, but so far she hadn't learned of anything too serious—which was just as well, since Chief O'Brien was presently aboard the *Rubicon* with Captain Sisko.

And in any case, most of those problems simply got in the way of more serious responsibilities, such as combing through all the data from the entire freighter incident, then doing it again in the hope of finding a clue they'd missed, something that might shed light on what had happened.

She glanced once more around Ops, observing the crew, all of whom were hard at work at their stations. Thank the Prophets for Dax. Kira had always been able to rely on Dax, both as a friend and as a science officer, and she was glad to have her here now, but she felt an added sense of assurance as she looked to Worf. She understood what it meant to be a warrior, a soldier, and to have that be the focus of your life . . . for a time. She knew the value of experience combined with expertise—which, she decided, was a fair description of DS9's Klingon Strategic Operations officer. As for the rest of the officers and personnel, they were some of the best Starfleet and Bajor had to offer, so there was reason to hope.

The station's shields and weapons systems checked out as fully operational, and for the moment at least, no one was threatening anyone on or near DS9. So there were things to be thankful for, she thought, as she turned her attention back to the main Ops table.

Using thrusters, the *Rubicon* headed toward unseen coordinates. Kira watched the runabout grow smaller as it moved slowly away from the station. She hadn't felt the urge to wave in years, but the memory brought a thin smile.

The intercom chirped. "Security to Major Kira." The voice was Odo's.

"Go ahead, Constable."

"We've had a disturbance on the Promenade. A fight broke out between the Aulep and the Rylep, but my men have it under control. I don't know if there are any serious injuries, I don't even know who started it yet, but in the meantime, I wondered if there was anything special you wanted me to do with them?"

"Just confine them to quarters for now."

"Very well, Major. Odo out."

"Rubicon to *Deep Space Nine,"* Sisko's voice broke in.

"Kira here," she said as the captain's face appeared on the screen.

"Major, take care of the place. We'll see you when we get back."

"Maybe our visitors will be through fighting with each other by then," Kira replied.

"Having a little . . . trouble?" Sisko asked.

Kira wrinkled her nose at him. "Oh, just a little," she said, trying to make light of it. The captain had enough on his mind right now. "Nothing we can't handle."

"Consider it a learning experience," Sisko said, letting a warm chuckle follow.

"Of course, neither of us has had enough of those," Kira said, as the captain's image disappeared. She watched the runabout vanished into the brilliant swirl of the wormhole, seeming to pull the wormhole after it and leaving only the darkness of space behind.

DS9 was Kira's station now, at least for a little while. She had a feeling she would be happy to hand it back to Sisko when he returned.

"We're on the other side of the wormhole," Jake told Elliena, as the stars filled their view through the runabout's tall front windows.

Elliena stared into space as if she were frozen in place. After a time she blinked and turned to him as if she had something to say, but she didn't speak. Jake tried to read her mood. Something like astonishment still filled her eyes, though he thought he saw a hint of terror there, too. He wasn't sure his own expression looked any more certain.

"Pretty amazing trip through the wormhole, wasn't it?" he said, trying to sound chatty.

"I've never seen anything like that," Elliena said, her voice a bit weak, but otherwise steady. She took a breath. "It is truly the home of the Prophets."

"Actually, my father helped prove that."

"The story of the Emissary is often told," Elliena said.

Jake nodded. They sat looking at the stars for a long, silent moment. Jake had learned some time ago that, especially for him, it was not a good idea to discuss religion with the Bajorans. Jake didn't think even his father knew quite where he fit into the Bajoran faith, or whether the aliens who had constructed the wormhole, and still lived within its strange dimensions, truly saw themselves as the gods of the Bajorans.

"I swear I didn't plan this," Jake said, grinning as she looked at him.

"I guess, maybe." Elliena returned the grin. She was playing, or trying to, Jake realized, which under the circumstances seemed like a good sign.

"I think we still have main power," he said. He tapped at the controls on the instrument panel. "I might be able to bring the engines back online and maybe get us out of here."

"Is there anything I can do?"

"You could watch those power grids," Jake suggested. He saw her eagerness to help as another good sign. She was trying to cope and doing a pretty good job of it so far. He felt determined not to let her down.

"We're not too badly damaged," Jake said after he had finished checking the primary systems. "At least not as far as I can tell. I've got us stabilized for now. I'll have to get a bearing and plot a course back through the wormhole, but if the main engines check out, we should be able to go to warp as soon as I—"

The shuttle jumped abruptly, then started shaking as if a giant hand had reached out and grabbed hold of it. Startled for a moment, Jake quickly came up with a better explanation.

"Another tractor beam," he told Elliena, grabbing hold of his chair to keep from being thrown from it. Elliena did the same.

He turned quickly to the controls and began active scanning. The display lit up almost instantly. The beam was easy enough to trace. He felt the bow coming around, lining up with the path of the beam.

"I've got its source pinpointed," he said. "Whatever it is, it should be coming into view in a few seconds."

Jake glanced at the image on the external monitor; it was small and vague but easy enough to identify: the Klingon freighter. He said nothing as the runabout rotated slightly to starboard. He didn't want to alarm Elliena.

"That looks like the same Klingon freighter that

got us into this mess," she said, her voice rising in panic.

"I know," he said. "I'll try hailing them."

"They didn't seem interested in talking just a little while ago."

"I know that, too," Jake said. "But it's worth trying."

He opened a channel. "This is Jake Sisko of the Federation runabout *Rio Grande*." He tried to think of the best way to phrase his next question, but he quickly gave up and kept it simple. "What do you want?"

There was no response. Jake hadn't really expected any. These Klingons had just destroyed one of their own ships and attacked DS9 before fleeing through the wormhole.

The runabout shook harder, turned a few more degrees, then calmed slightly as Jake released it from station keeping. He let the tractor beam dictate the runabout's new heading.

"Where do you think they're taking us?" Elliena asked, sounding nervous now. It was already clear they that were not headed back toward the wormhole.

"I don't know," Jake said. He took her left hand and held it gently in his. "But we'll be all right, I know we will." He tried another grin. "Hey, this isn't the first time I've had to deal with this kind of thing."

"What kind of thing?"

"The unknown," Jake said. "Or worse. There's

usually a way to deal with any situation. We need time, that's the main thing. Somebody will come after us sooner or later. All we have to do is stay calm and in one piece until then. We can do that. I promise you, Elliena, I won't let anything happen to you."

"You don't have to promise," Elliena told him, looking at him with big round eyes. "And you don't have to spend all your time trying to comfort me, either. I may not have much experience with space travel or with Klingons, but I'm a fast learner. I know a little something about Cardassians, and I understand that they aren't all that different from Klingons, when you get down to it."

Jake watched her, trying to guess how she meant all of that—whether he'd made her feel like a child. He hadn't meant to.

She seemed to read his thoughts. "Don't worry," she said softly, smiling at him now. "I took it the right way."

"Good," Jake said with relief.

The runabout shook again, bringing back thoughts of the worst, thoughts Jake was trying to banish. "What I meant was that I feel responsible for getting you into this. But whatever happens—"

"I know, and I'm all right," Elliena said. "After all, I asked to go on a runabout with you, remember? This was as much my idea as it was yours. But I have to admit, this is more adventure than I bargained for."

"Actually, I take back what I said before, about

how I didn't plan this. Actually, I *did* plan the whole thing—just so we could be alone." Jake peeked out at her from under a lowered brow, hoping to lighten a grave situation.

Elliena made a sour face, but then she squeezed his hand. "You probably did, at that."

"My father would tell us to look at this as a learning experience," Jake said.

"I'll try. I just hope it isn't the last experience we ever have."

Jake looked up again, then gazed out through the windows. His breath caught in his throat as his eyes went wide. The ship tractoring them had changed; it wasn't Klingon anymore.

"Computer," Jake said, "identify the ship directly off our bow."

"Sensor readings inconclusive," the computer replied. "Ship configuration consistent with a Federation runabout."

"Even I can see that," Elliena told him, looking out in shared amazement. "It looks just like the ship we're on."

Shaking his head, Jake took a moment to review the sensor readings. He didn't have enough expertise, he knew that, but from what he could gather, the sensors weren't picking up the other runabout at all, at least not in any way he would have expected. He noticed trace energy readings, just as he had when the Klingon freighter was there only moments ago, but nothing else.

The tractor beam was still attached, however.

There was no question why the helm wasn't answering.

"Computer, maximum magnification." Jake glanced at Elliena. "I want to get a closer look at that ship."

The image on the runabout's small viewscreen was replaced by that of a hull at close proximity. The area that was displayed was small, but part of the runabout's identification markings were visible.

"Look," Jake said, pointing.

Elliena squinted, then shrugged. "I can't read it. The image is too blurry."

"I know, but the rest of the image is perfectly focused."

"So what's that mean?"

"I don't know. It's just odd, that's all."

They sat patiently for a while, watching, worrying all the more. Jake let the time add up to an hour. Then he began to feel the full frustration of their dilemma. He turned toward Elliena, seriously considering at least one of their options. "We still have the weapons systems," he whispered, as though the other runabout might hear him, even though he had closed all communications channels.

Elliena looked stricken. "I don't think fighting that ship is such a good idea, no matter what it looks like. You saw what happened to the other freighter."

"I know, but the farther we're dragged away from the wormhole, the harder it will be for anyone from the station to find us. We can't just sit here and let that ship drag us all over the Gamma Quadrant."

"I suppose not," Elliena complained. "But I definitely don't want to fight them."

"Me either. But I've been giving this a lot of thought. That tractor beam should be an easy target at this range. With the help of the computer, maybe we could knock the beam emitter out, then go to warp before the other ship has time to react. I'd have to get the engines online and ready first, then lay in a course and raise the shields."

"Sounds like something out of one of our stories about the freedom fighters."

"I think it's what Major Kira or my father would do."

"If you really think so."

Jake realized all the color had drained from Elliena's face. She had to be scared half to death, he knew. He swallowed, deciding he'd have to be brave enough for both of them. Without another word he went to work. He wasn't sure he'd be able to accomplish all the tasks he'd set for himself, but in just a few minutes he had managed. The only uncertainty was the course he'd selected, but he decided even that was close enough.

"Computer, lock phasers on to the source of that tractor beam." Jake paused, holding his breath. The warp engines waited at his fingertips.

"I guess you know what you're doing, but you can tell me again if you like," Elliena said evenly.

He knew what she meant. "Engaging warp engines. Firing phasers—now!"

Jake watched as the phaser beam lit the darkness,

then passed right through the other runabout. The tractor beam was still holding. A split second later a series of energy beams lashed out from the other ship and struck the *Rio Grande*'s shields. The ship jumped, then pitched from the impacts of the beams. The other ship fired again, and half the instrument consoles flared with excess energy, then went dark. Jake jabbed chaotically at panels. Nothing worked. Main power was out, along with the sensors and the weapons systems. He didn't know if they had any shields left.

When he looked up, the other runabout was out of view again, but he knew it was still there, still pulling at them with its tractor beam. After a few seconds he decided they probably weren't going to fire again.

"I guess I shouldn't have done that," he muttered.

"Another learning experience," Elliena said. She leaned toward him and put her hand on his.

Jake looked at her. He knew how she meant that, too. "All we've learned so far is that I'm too stupid to take my own advice."

"Berating yourself won't help."

Jake shrugged. "There isn't much else to do."

"What happened to the guy who told me we'd be all right?"

"Oh, he's here somewhere."

"Go get him. I liked him better."

Jake took her hand between his. In a way, she was holding up better than he was. Which he thought was just fine.

"I can do that," he said.

"I know." Elliena smiled at him, a look that made Jake feel as if he could save the universe. But he decided to set his sights a bit lower. *I won't let you down,* he vowed in silence. He was sure of that much.

"So what do we do now?" Elliena asked.

"We go back to waiting. We're being taken somewhere for some reason. Until we learn more, we can't make any plans."

Elliena pursed her lips and nodded; Jake was glad to see her determined look. They kept hold of each other's hands and watched the stars appear to drift. Jake guessed the runabout must be traveling at close to maximum impulse speed. Then their view through the windows began to cloud, as if a thick gaseous curtain were being drawn over the ship.

"I think we're entering an atmosphere," Elliena said, peering out the window.

"I don't think so, at least not any kind of atmosphere I'm familiar with. It's like pea soup out there."

"What kind of soup?"

"Something my father likes. I'll have him fix you some when we get back."

The view beyond the windows grew darker until nothing at all could be seen. Jake held Elliena's hand tighter as he continued to peer into the nothingness outside. He had almost no sensation of motion anymore and no instruments to inform him of what his senses could not perceive. What he'd told Elliena was true: he had faced the unknown before, but never anything quite like this. He swallowed. *I can handle this,* he told himself.

At length the runabout swayed several times, then surged, like a boat caught in a sudden storm. Then the hull bumped into something solid and came to a stop.

CHAPTER
10

"I'VE GOT A READING, Captain," O'Brien said, glancing up from his console. "It's pretty faint, but it's identical to the neutrino trail on our side of the wormhole."

"Good," Sisko said. He forced himself to remain calm and steady. "Lay in a course along its trajectory. Let's see where it takes us." He examined his own console as he switched scanning modes. "I'm not picking up anything on the long-range sensors."

O'Brien took a moment to look over Sisko's readings, then compared headings. "No, but it looks as if this course is going to take us through the Myalon Corridor."

Sisko nodded with mild satisfaction as the runabout came around, then began accelerating to near maximum warp speeds, leaving the "real" universe behind. That was something positive, at least.

O'Brien went on, "I was hoping the *Rio Grande* would be sitting here just waiting for us when we came out of the wormhole."

"So was I," Sisko said, "but we'll have to take what we can get, for now."

"Sir," O'Brien said after a moment, "suppose that freighter did go into the wormhole after Jake and Elliena. What do you think the Klingons would want with a couple of kids and a Starfleet runabout?"

"We don't know for sure that the Klingons went after anyone, or even that the captors were Klingons. We can't assume anything at this point."

"No, but somebody has those kids, or they'd have been here. And whoever the captors are, they're more than just a projection of some kind."

"When we catch up to them we'll have to ask a few questions," Sisko said, looking at O'Brien. "Right after we get Jake and Elliena back."

The chief didn't ask how Sisko planned to accomplish that; Sisko hadn't expected him to. Neither of them had any specific ideas, he knew, only the determination and, he hoped, the experience to do the right thing at the right time. For now they had to sit back and wait.

Which was precisely what they did for the next several hours. They took turns watching the sensor displays, monitoring the runabout's heading, and double-checking the computer. The trail they were following had all but disappeared, but they kept on course, agreeing that it was the only reasonable alternative . . . even though they didn't seem to be getting results.

Sisko found himself dreaming, as he rested during the chief's watch, that O'Brien was waking him up, telling him he'd found something.

"I'm getting a contact, maximum range," O'Brien reported. "Reading a large spherical mass, moving at nominal speed. Probably that planetoid Dax told us about."

Sisko blinked and realized it wasn't a dream at all. "What's the status of our trail of neutrinos?" he asked, sitting up, shaking the last vestiges of sleep from his mind.

"I've got what I think is the same trail, though there aren't enough particles to be sure. It seems to be leading toward the same coordinates. Of course, it could go right past the planet, just like we're about to."

Sisko nodded as he checked the scanning displays. He verified what O'Brien had told him, but didn't come up with anything else. He frowned. Where could Jake and Elliena be?

"We'll continue on our present course. That should take us close enough to get a good scan."

O'Brien nodded, then waited as the distance between the *Rubicon* and the contact narrowed, allowing more information to become available. "It's a spherical planetoid," he said finally. "No orbital companions, but . . ." He made a face as he went silent.

Sisko studied the same readings as they drew to within full sensor range, and he realized what had silenced the chief. The readings just didn't make sense. Could the sensors be malfunctioning?

"What do you make of it?" Sisko asked.

"I don't know," the chief said. "According to these readings, that planet is more biological than mineral. I'm detecting large amounts of carbon laced with complex organic compounds."

"Not exactly the kind of biology I'm familiar with," Sisko said. "Is it possible we're picking up surface readings, some sort of plant life, perhaps, covering the entire surface?"

"The overall biomass is too great for that. That thing is only three-quarters the size of Earth's moon. Even if it was completely covered with vegetation, that wouldn't be enough to account for this much organic substance. Besides, there isn't any sun to keep the planetoid warm enough for life as we know it to exist to exist on its surface. Thermal vents could account for some of it the plant life, but again, we'd be talking isolated pockets."

"We're going to investigate a little further," Sisko said. "If that planetoid has a surface, Jake may have landed there."

"Or been taken there."

Sisko nodded heavily, thinking the same thing.

As the planetoid came into view, Sisko and O'Brien continued to analyze the sensor data. Only new questions arose.

"I'm not detecting any life-forms on the surface," O'Brien reported. "Just dense gas—hydrogen, methane, ammonia. It's a pretty nasty place."

"And there's no trace of the *Rio Grande*," Sisko said grimly. He hesitated. His every instinct said to check out the planetoid. But what if he was wrong?

"Captain, if Jake and Elliena crashed down there, they wouldn't have lasted very long," O'Brien said, only stating the obvious. "The slightest breach in their hull would have done them in." Then, as if to offer his captain some hope, he continued, "On the other hand, it takes quite a bit of doing to breach one of these hulls."

"I know. Thanks, Chief," Sisko said with a wry smile. Then he changed the subject: "Any change in the neutrino trail?"

"Too diffuse to follow, but from what I can tell, it hasn't varied from its course since we started tracking it. We could continue on our projected course."

"I agree."

"For all we know, this may be as far as the neutrino trail goes, and there may not be anything out here other than that little planet. Before we run off, though, I think we should make absolutely certain nothing's there."

Sisko nodded. "Plot a search grid. We'll reconfigure the sensors for optimum penetration of the atmosphere, then try to cover every inch of that planet."

"I'll set the computer for the widest possible parameters, but we'll have to keep watch for about three hours. The runabout might not be the only thing down there, and if that's the case, well, we don't know what else we're likely to find."

Sisko put the *Rubicon* into a low orbit around the planetoid while O'Brien initiated the computer-guided search pattern. Multiple fluctuating energy signatures began to register almost at once, but they were too numerous and random to allow O'Brien and Sisko to speculate. They would just have to wait.

After more than two hours, the sensors had identified dozens of increasingly active EM impulse clusters scattered all through the sphere, but there was still no sign of the runabout, Sisko thought with increasing frustration. Had they been wasting their time?

Sisko watched an especially active pulse work its way across hundreds of kilometers of surface in a strangely erratic zigzag pattern, then plunge straight down into the planet. A second later another small cluster of pulses raced along nearly the same path, as if chasing the first, then vanished at nearly the same spot. There was no way of knowing whether the pulses kept going through the interior of the planet, but he had a hunch that they did.

"Can you make anything of that?" he asked, after he and O'Brien had watched half a dozen smaller plasma trails scurry across the sensor displays and vanish into the depths of the clouded surface below.

O'Brien shook his head. "No, sir, nothing definite. But my guess is they're electrical storms of some kind. They'd have to be, though I've never seen storms act quite like this, and the patterns don't fit any known phenomenon in the computer records."

"It does remind me of something, though," Sisko reflected, resting his chin on his right hand as he continued to stare at the consoles. What was it? If only he wasn't so worried about Jake.

O'Brien waited a moment. "Of what?"

"That's just it, I don't remember. But it'll come to me."

The external warning klaxon suddenly began buzzing. O'Brien instantly began studying the tactical displays. "I'm barely reading anything, but there is something out there," he reported.

Sisko logged the coordinates, then put the image on the viewscreen. "It's another ship," he said. "And it's making a fast approach."

"I can't get any identification," O'Brien said. "But my guess is we've found that phantom Klingon freighter again."

"Or it's found us. In any case, the approaching ship is too big to be the *Rio Grande*."

"I agree," O'Brien said grimly. "Whoever it is, they're doing zero point nine nine light-speed, but I'm not reading any impulse drive signature."

"All right," Sisko said, as a sense of uneasy satisfaction quickened his pulse. "Shields up. Let's not give them any opportunities."

Sisko tapped his screen controls to magnify the image in an attempt to see full detail, but at first there wasn't any. The huge vessel blurred before his eyes, and then hard lines began to emerge, revealing that this ship was considerably smaller than the last one. What finally emerged was a Federation runabout—but it wasn't the *Rio Grande*.

"It looks like the *Rubicon*," O'Brien said, shaking his head. "In fact, it's practically identical. Otherwise it reads the same as the second Klingon freighter did back at the station."

"No solid mass," Sisko said.

"Aye. Only very faint energy readings."

"It's there . . . but it isn't."

"Yes, sir. And it's heading straight toward us."

CHAPTER
11

"YOU CAN'T BE SERIOUS!" Kira said, planting both hands on her hips and glaring at the Tellarite trader standing before her on the Promenade.

"I can be anything you want me to be," the alien replied, tilting his bearded face to one side, wrinkling his snout and bushy eyebrows, as if he were sniffing at her.

"Okay, how about being a gentleman?" Kira made sure he read the aggravation in her voice.

"If you prefer, but the unfortunate fact is that I will be on *Deep Space Nine* for only a very short time, and I have never engaged in any form of mating behavior with a Bajoran woman. And, as I mentioned, I have been told by many that you are as fine a specimen as I am likely to find."

Kira rolled her eyes. She had spent the morning

putting out "fires" all over the station. The troublesome situations had ranged from a suspected contraband cargo on a transport that had just docked to a medical emergency involving a small fleet of runabout-size ships with crew members who were sick with an unknown fever for which Dr. Bashir had so far been unable to devise a treatment. To add to her problems, repairs of the damage caused by the Klingon freighter explosion were going slowly, causing a cascade of other delays.

And now she was being propositioned by a . . . a pig!

But enough was enough.

She leaned toward the Tellarite, dropping her air of abashment and wrinkling her own nose, adding a sniff as she scowled at him. The smell of some pungent, sour herb was apparently emanating from every pore in his thick skin. "I do appreciate the compliment," she said. "And as this is your first visit, I want to assure you that it is my intention as acting commander of this station to make everyone's stay here as comfortable and . . . amicable as possible, but I must offer just one warning."

"Of course!"

"If you ever put your hands on me again"—she glanced down, checking his extremities—"I will personally—"

"Confine you to your ship," Odo finished from just behind her. She turned and looked at him steadily, holding her tongue.

"I'm sure that's what you were going to say," Odo added.

"That is *exactly* what I was going to say," Kira said through clenched teeth.

"Of course," Odo said. Then he turned a harsh eye to the Tellarite. "Now, move along."

"I don't like threats," the visitor said.

Odo smiled at him. "I don't make threats."

At this, the Tellarite did as he'd been told. Kira gave a low snort. All bluster and no bite, she decided. Just as well; she had enough on her hands right now.

"Thanks, Odo," Kira said with a sigh. "It's barely noon, and I'm ready to rip people's heads off."

"I know the feeling, Major. I'm glad I could help. I was looking for you for a reason, though. A group of Bajoran university students would like to spend a day touring the station. They're asking if they can come tomorrow."

"Tomorrow?" Kira balked.

"Under the circumstances I suggested that they postpone their visit for a few days, at least until we complete repairs and settle this Rylep-Aulep situation."

"I agree. I don't think we've even got docking space for them right now. And we still don't know why we were attacked by that vanishing Klingon freighter. For all we know, it might even come back. The Klingons themselves haven't responded to our requests for information."

"So I've heard," Odo said.

Kira's comm badge chirped once.

"Ops to Major Kira." It was Dax.

"Go ahead."

"We need you up here right away. We've got more company coming."

Kira took a breath, held it. How bad could it be? she kidded herself halfheartedly.

"I'll be right there."

As Kira entered Ops, she heard Commander Worf's deep voice: "Identity confirmed."

That's a good start, she thought. "Status?" she asked.

"Two ships approaching at warp speed," Dax said.

"Put them on the screen," Kira said.

"Both are Klingon, a Bird of Prey and a Vor'cha-class attack cruiser," Worf continued. "They are dropping to impulse, and both have shields up."

Kira eyed the screen. "Are their weapons armed?"

Worf ran the scan. "Not yet."

"Assume an identical posture," Kira ordered.

"They're hailing us," Dax said.

Kira nodded. The image of the two vessels on the screen was suddenly replaced by the dark, bearded face of a stocky middle-aged Klingon.

"I am Drokas," the commander said. "I have been sent by the High Council to determine precisely what has happened to our freighter. I will hear your explanation now."

"I assure you, Commander," Kira told him, "we

136

would like an explanation as well. We don't have one. Perhaps you can help us find the answers."

"And I can assure you, Major, I did not come here to be played with. Gowron will not be pleased with anything less than the truth."

Kira nodded. She had a feeling that the truth, whatever it was, wouldn't make Gowron any happier. "We are still trying to determine what happened," she said. "Can you tell us what mission your freighters were on, where they might have come from, and what sort of special technologies the second freighter was utilizing? I wasn't aware you were outfitting cargo vessels with an experimental cloaking device."

"Enough!" Drokas snarled, glaring at her. "You are speaking nonsense. There was but one freighter, and it had no special technologies. I do not know what your game is, Major, but I have no intention of playing it."

Kira considered the possibility that Drokas really didn't know much more than she did. She tried to think of an approach that wouldn't make her look like a fool but would keep the Klingon commander talking. She considered letting Worf handle the situation, but she'd started this, and she wanted to finish it. In any case, Commander Worf and the House of Gowron were not on the best of terms. No, she decided, it was best to keep things open and honest.

"I'll make you a deal, Drokas. You tell me what

you know, and I'll tell you what I know—which, I'll warn you, isn't much. No nonsense, no games. We didn't do anything to your ships, and we're just as concerned as you are."

Drokas looked at her from the screen for a long moment, moving his eyes only slightly; then he took a shallow breath. "We received a distress call from Captain Dolras of the freighter *Toknor*. He indicated they were under attack at *Deep Space Nine*. Then we lost the signal. We scanned the debris near this station, and we know it came from the *Toknor*."

Kira nodded briskly. "Your freighter came through the wormhole from the Gamma Quadrant. It was followed moments later by another, identical Klingon freighter. The *Toknor* was already heavily damaged; then the second freighter destroyed it. After that it just . . . disappeared. We think it may have gone back through the wormhole, but we have no way of knowing for sure."

"Freighters do not disappear," Drokas snapped, the sound of rage coloring his voice.

Kira explained the unusual sensor readings, or the lack of them, and the way the second freighter had faded until it vanished like a ghost into nothingness.

"A fascinating story, Major, but Klingons do not believe in ghost ships," Drokas said, frowning. "I believe none of this!"

"She is telling the truth," Worf said.

"Ahh, now I am to believe a traitor," Drokas replied to Worf directly, narrowing his eyes. The two

Klingons glared at each other. Kira glanced at Dax, who shook her head discreetly.

"We can make our sensor logs available to you," Kira said. "You can see for yourself."

"Sensor logs can be manufactured almost as easily as your stories," Drokas said. "Tell me, Major, why you sent one of your runabouts through the wormhole almost immediately after the destruction of our freighter."

Kira didn't know how Drokas knew, but she was certain that lately the Klingon Empire had been keeping a close eye on DS9, much as the Cardassians had. She took a deep breath. "That information isn't relevant."

"Ah, but it might be, Major," Drokas said with a sudden slight grin, a predatory look that offered no comfort. "If some of the crew escaped the *Toknor* in life pods before it was destroyed, then went back through the wormhole, your runabout could have been sent to finish the job so the survivors could not talk."

"The runabout is part of a rescue mission," Kira said, putting an equal measure of sarcasm in her own voice now. "There were civilians lost in the attack whom we are attempting to locate. Bajoran and Federation civilians, not Klingons. But we're still talking about what I know. You haven't told me about the Toknor's mission."

"And I will not!" Drokas shouted, leaning forward in his chair. The shadows deepened between the ridges on his forehead. "It is of no consequence. There was no second Klingon ship, ghost or real, and we both know it. I do not believe your report, Major, and neither will Gowron. He is not amused by either Federation treachery or Bajoran lies. When he hears of this, you will realize the gravity of your error."

With a violent wave of his hand toward one of his officers, Drokas broke contact.

Kira looked first to Worf, then to Dax. Neither of them had any comment.

"Well, I tried," Kira said heavily. Why were things always so complicated?

She turned back to Worf. "Keep those shields up, Commander. And you'd better power up some of our phasers, just in case."

"That may not be necessary," Worf replied, tapping at his consoles, observing the results. "Both cruisers are engaging thrusters. They are moving off."

Kira breathed a little easier.

"It's unlikely that they will just give up," Dax said.

Kira nodded in agreement, but as she looked at the main screen she understood. The Klingons weren't giving up. They planned to check out her story for themselves. She watched as the two Klingon warships came slowly about, then moved toward the wormhole's coordinates, causing it to materialize. A moment later both ships vanished.

"Just as well," Worf grumbled, frowning at the screen as the brightly swirling wormhole vanished.

"Perhaps," Kira reflected. "But not necessarily."

"Major, Dr. Bashir would like to see you as soon as possible," Dax said.

Kira looked up. "What now?"

"Security has just reported another brawl on the Promenade," Worf said. "I suspect it may have something to do with the earlier fight."

Kira was already heading for the turbolift. "You're probably right. Tell him I'll be right there."

She found Odo waiting for her in the infirmary. Just as she'd suspected, the Aulep and the Rylep had gotten out of their quarters and gone at it again. This time, however, the fight had grown big enough and gone far enough to leave a legacy of injuries ranging from concussions to broken bones. Unfortunately, some of the casualties were visiting traders and station security personnel.

"I've treated most of the injured," Bashir told her, stepping away from his medical consoles. The expression on his young, slender face lacked its usual enthusiasm. In fact, Kira thought, he looked downright annoyed.

"We had quite a time at first, trying to keep the combatants separated. It's a little difficult to tell Aulep and Rylep apart when you're in a hurry."

"I'm sure it is," Kira said.

"So," the doctor went on, "should I expect many more casualties?"

Kira shrugged. "I hope not. But then, I didn't think we'd end up in this situation to begin with."

"I've tightened security considerably, Doctor," Odo said, his smooth, molded face utterly neutral. "Things should stay quiet for a while."

Kira looked around the infirmary. The injured lay on biobeds, some of them under scanners that covered nearly half their torsos. The whole situation with these visitors had gotten out of hand; it could no longer await attention. "I want to see the Rylep and Aulep commanders in the conference room in one hour, provided they are able. Quark, too."

Odo nodded.

"We're going to settle this," Kira said, "one way or another."

"Thieves!"

"Murderers!"

"Somehow I don't think we're making any real progress," Kira said, interrupting the all-too-familiar exchange between Dorram and Flenn.

"He is intractable," Flenn said of Dorram.

"*He* is intractable!" Dorram snarled back. He had a sizable bruise over his right eye, and Flenn was favoring one entire side of his body. Kira wondered briefly what the extent of their injuries had been before Dr. Bashir worked on the two of them.

"What you both must realize," she went on nobly, "is that neither of you will be allowed to leave this station—or your secured quarters, for that matter—until we make some kind of lasting progress here. You must put aside your differences, start fresh, and look for solutions instead of problems." She had been rehearsing this speech for the past hour, hoping to appeal to their better nature. She wasn't certain how small a target she was aiming for.

"In other words," Odo said, following Kira's request that he jump in anywhere he could, "try calling it even."

"Even?" Flenn said, his round eyes getting rounder.

Dorram and Flenn stared at each other as if aglow in the light of sudden revelation.

"Yes," Odo said, glancing at Kira, *"even* if you don't want to."

"I think the major and Odo are making sense," Quark added, nodding agreeably but proving to be of little help otherwise.

Kira opened her mouth to speak, but the chirp of her comm badge cut her off.

"Kira here," she answered.

"Major," the voice of Commander Worf came back, "you are needed in Ops again."

"Now what?" Kira moaned. "I'm in the middle of a meeting, Commander."

"Several unidentified ships are coming through the wormhole. We are attempting to hail them. No response as yet."

"I see," Kira said, already starting toward the conference room door. She paused and turned a cold eye on Flenn, Dorram, and Quark, who were staring at her, closemouthed.

"I don't suppose any of you have anything you'd like to say?"

All three heads moved slowly from side to side.

"I didn't think so," Kira said, moving staunchly toward the door. "You'll excuse me," she finished, and let the door slip shut behind her.

She arrived in Ops a moment later.

"We are detecting three ships decelerating toward the station," Worf reported. "Similar but unknown configurations. Still no response to our hails."

Kira watched the screen as it filled with the images of the approaching vessels. These were nearly twice the size of the Aulep and Rylep ships, but much cruder in appearance. Nevertheless, Dax confirmed that the drive sections were of the same type.

Slowly, weapons systems armed, the three ships took up offensive positions around DS9, placing the station within a precisely measured triangle.

"They seem to be targeting the station's core area and the visiting Aulep and Rylep vessels," Worf reported.

"Opinions?" Kira asked, glancing from station to station.

"I'd say they're some sort of all-purpose vessel," Dax responded, "passenger or freight, though from what I can read of their holds, they aren't carrying much of either. Otherwise we're looking at some pretty basic equipment. And they're slow, no more than warp four or five, I would guess."

"Each ship has a single large disrupter-type weapon," Worf pointed out. "I estimate all the ships' energy resources must be used to fire their weapons, but together they have sufficient firepower to pose a serious threat, unless of course we neutralize them first."

"Major, they're hailing," Dax said.

"Good," Kira said. "Let's find out what they want."

The face on the screen was humanoid and apparently male. Vivid green eyes, a wide jaw, and a thin, straight nose completed his gaunt features. A floppy hat made of soft, dark material covered most of his head, and long grayish hair hung down around his shoulders. His thin, slightly wrinkled neck disappeared abruptly into a stiff, seamless collar decorated with gold piping.

"I am Bedal, of the Beshiel Second Realm."

"Major Kira Nerys of Bajor, acting commander of *Deep Space Nine*."

The alien wasn't impressed. "We expect your full cooperation, or the consequences will be dire and immediate."

"This is getting a bit monotonous," Dax remarked half under her breath.

"Cooperation in what?" Kira asked.

"You know very well," Bedal replied.

Kira tried to shake off the annoyance that was beginning to cloud her thoughts. "I am afraid I do not," she replied, speaking each word slowly and clearly.

"We have come for our stolen trellium crystals, and we will not leave without them."

"The Aulep's crystals?" Kira asked, somewhat astonished.

"Or the Rylep's crystals, depending on whose story you wish to believe," Worf reminded her.

"They belong to us!" Bedal insisted quite angrily. "As does vengeance for the crimes committed against all Beshiel by those to whom you have chosen to grant sanctuary."

"Of course." Kira looked away from the screen. What would Captain Sisko do under these circumstances? She decided to start over. Steadily she began, "We have granted sanctuary to no one. We are a neutral station. You are in Bajoran space, however, and you will be held accountable for your actions."

"And what of these thieves you harbor? Who will hold them responsible for *their* actions?"

"Suppose you explain your accusations," Kira said as gently as possible. "We need to understand the situation in order to act responsibly, and we know almost as little about the Aulep and the Rylep as we know about you."

"A cultural exchange will have to wait until a more appropriate time," Bedal replied. "As to our mission here, I can explain quickly enough. Our system is rich in minerals, a fact that is well known in our region of the galaxy. These resources have helped us prosper for centuries, but we work very hard to extract and refine those riches." He indicated the Aulep and Rylep ships. "Some, like the criminals you are currently protecting on your station, would take an easier route."

"You have proof of this?"

"We do."

"One moment, please," Kira said. She motioned for Dax to mute the channel, then tapped her comm badge. "Kira to Odo." She waited only a second before she received Odo's response. "Get Quark and those other two up here on the double."

"It will be my pleasure, Major," Odo replied.

With the channel open again she turned once more to the Beshiel. "I'm not sure what you plan to do now," she began, "but let me offer a possible course—"

"We intend to get our crystals back and see these thieves brought to justice. Failing that, we intend to see them destroyed, and you along with them. You leave us no other choice in the matter." Bedal sounded as if the moment's respite had fired his fury still further. Or perhaps, Kira speculated, he was attempting to screen his fears.

"Again I assure you that we had nothing to do with creating your problems, and we are willing to attempt to help solve them . . . somehow. But I would like to work this out peaceably, Bedal. All of us: you, me, the Aulep, and the Rylep."

"Why should we trust you?" Bedal said, sounding not the least bit conciliatory. "We have followed these thieves for days, hoping to find out who their buyers were, so that we could stop them. We thought we had lost them until we learned of the wormhole. Now finally we find them here under your protection. The Aulep and Rylep ships outrun us, in battle their weapons are superior to ours, and their raids outwit our security time and again. Recently they have somehow managed to capture one of our own ships, and have used it to get close to us and our outposts with impunity. When we finally determine the ship is not a genuine Beshiel, they attack. One of our ships has been completely destroyed along with its full crew! It is possible that *you* are the buyers and would do or say anything to keep your options open."

"I can see how you'd feel that way," Kira told him. "But surely we can all sit down together and work this out."

"I do not think so," Bedal said calmly. "If the Aulep or the Rylep promise anything, they will break that promise. If they go away, they will come back. The solution must be a permanent one. An example must be made, and their buyers must be eliminated. We must act here and now! Their friends are our enemies. And until I have proof to the contrary, we must consider you their friends!"

The turbolift reached Ops. Kira watched as Quark, Flenn, and Dorram stepped off and were ushered ahead by Odo. By the time they reached Kira's side it was clear to her that Flenn and Dorram recognized the face that appeared on the main viewscreen. They looked about to choke.

"Destroy them immediately!" Flenn shouted.

"Before it is too late!" Dorram added in haste.

"There are three ships out there," Kira replied, "all from the Beshiel Second Realm. Are you suggesting I destroy all three of them, or should I take their advice and let them do as they wish with the two of you?"

"Destroy all three ships!" Flenn cried out.

"Yes, all of them!" Dorram said.

"Well, it's nice to see they can finally agree on something," Odo said.

Kira fixed first Flenn and then Dorram with a penetrating stare. "It's not that simple," she said. "You see, they have an interesting story to tell. They say you've taken advantage of them."

"Hardly!" Flenn insisted.

"Don't listen to them," Dorram said. "They are treacherous. They have gone so far as to build ships that look like ours in order to attack us with impunity!"

"And they build ships like ours!" Flenn said.

"Now you accuse us of your own tricks," Bedal snarled from the screen. "But your kind are always lying, and of course you are both lying now!"

"Major," Worf said, looking up from his tactical station. "Another ship is approaching from Federation space; it is about to drop out of warp. Incoming message . . . they are demanding permission to dock."

"Demanding?" Dax repeated, raising an eyebrow to Worf.

"In the name of the Prophets!" Kira said. Would this nightmare never end? "What now?"

"I have identification," Worf replied. "It is a Ferengi Marauder."

Kira felt the tension in her forehead turning into a

terrific headache. "Ferengi?" she said. She spun around to face Quark. "Would you care to speculate?" she asked, taking a step toward him, changing her expression to one of extreme . . . sincerity.

Quark swallowed hard. "Well . . ." he began.

"Let me guess," Odo said. "They're the buyers, right?"

Quark, Kira thought, seemed suddenly to grow just a bit shorter. Slowly he began to nod.

"That's something I didn't need to hear," Kira muttered. She had thought that the many years she'd spent risking her life fighting in the Bajoran underground had prepared her for almost anything, but she had never imagined a day quite like this one. "Very well," she said dully. "Let's open a channel."

"I'm putting DaiMon Klarn, the commander of the Ferengi ship, on the main viewscreen," Dax said.

Kira waved a limp hand at the screen, then watched as the bumpy forehead and large ears of the Marauder's commander appeared. He looked irate.

"Welcome to *Deep Space Nine,*" Kira began. "I am Major Kira Nerys, acting commander—"

"I demand to talk to Quark!" Klarn said, nearly growling as he cut Kira off.

"Major, the Ferengi have raised their shields," Worf informed her.

Kira snatched a breath. "You know, I never get to finish my introductions lately." She turned to where Quark had been a moment ago, only to see he wasn't there anymore. She scanned the rest of Ops and finally spotted him standing directly behind Commander Worf, just out of sight of the screen.

"Very well, DaiMon Klarn," Kira began. "As a matter of fact, I'd like nothing better than—"

"I did not ask to talk to you, female," Klarn interrupted again, scowling condescendingly, showing Kira a mouthful of uneven, pointed teeth. "I asked for Quark!"

With that Klarn pounded one fist on the arm of his command chair. Then he leaned forward. "We are already two days behind schedule, and still Quark sends messages that ask us to wait even longer. I do not know what problems exist, for Quark or for anyone else, and I do not care. I am tired of delays and excuses, and I will tolerate not one more. Do I make myself clear? Now, where is he!"

"Wetting his pants," Dax said under her breath. Kira glanced at her, and a small fraction of the moment's burdens seemed to go away. Then she looked back to the screen.

"DaiMon Klarn, we are busy here at the moment, as you can clearly see. Or perhaps you are unaware that the three Beshiel ships circling the station with you have their weapons armed and trained on us and are apparently about to attempt to destroy the station and everyone in its vicinity. Possibly including you. Now, I'm sure all your problems with Quark can be worked out. However, you need to give us time to settle the Beshiel matter first."

"No, I don't think so," Klarn said. Kira noticed that he was beginning to fidget now, his eyes and fingers restless. "I have waited a long time for a truly profitable opportunity such as this one. That is why I am here. And I do not intend to listen to more lies or to wait any longer. If you are having difficulties with other races, that does not concern me in the least. I will not be kept from my merchandise another moment!"

"We cannot afford to drop our shields long enough to allow you to dock or to transport any merchandise you might be owed," Kira stated flatly. "In case you haven't noticed, there is a small fleet of ships prepared to open fire on us." She locked stares with Klarn again. "And I don't think you want to take that kind of risk, do you? It is in your best interest to let me try to resolve that situation before dealing with yours."

"If I have to open fire on these Beshiel friends of yours to get to my crystals, I'll do it!" Klarn came back. "Don't think I won't!"

Kira stood silent as the Ferengi commander turned and gave the order to train the Marauder's formidable weapons on the Beshiel. Then Klarn looked at Kira through the screen again, but continued speaking to his own crew.

"Hail the Beshiel," he said. He paused, then took a breath. "I am DaiMon Klarn of the Ferengi," he told them. "You will stand down at once. We are here to take delivery of a shipment of crystals. We have no part in your quarrel, but I am not a tolerant man, and I have no time for delays. As soon as we are gone, you can do what you want to whomever you want, but until then, anyone who interferes with my mission will suffer the most dire consequences!"

"I'm afraid the Beshiel's quarrel may have more to do with you than you think," Kira said humorlessly.

"Explain," Klarn demanded.

Kira and Odo looked at each other, as did Dax and Worf. Then all four of them deferred to Quark, who—with a strong assist from one of Worf's large hands—reluctantly stumbled into the open. He raised his eyes to the viewscreen.

"Quark, is that you?" Klarn boomed, leaning forward again in his chair, his wide, grooved nose nearly filling the screen.

Quark nodded.

"Finally!" Klarn said. "Now, where are my crystals!"

"It seems . . ." Quark said, his voice starting to crack, "it seems there's a small . . . *problem.*"

CHAPTER
12

"ANY LIFE SIGNS?" Sisko asked, studying the image of the newly arrived phantom *Rubicon,* which was closing in on them.

"Negative," O'Brien said. "Nothing recognizable, and no hull echoes, just faint energy traces."

Sisko checked their stats. They were maintaining a high orbit around the slowly spinning planetoid, but they hadn't had time to do an extensive investigation of the sphere itself. And it looked as if they might not get the chance.

"We must consider them hostile," Sisko said. "We still don't know why that look-alike Klingon freighter fired on the *Toknor,* so we have to assume this runabout double might fire on us."

"I don't think starting a fight with them is a good

idea," O'Brien said. "We should think about leaving orbit and going to warp."

"Do you think that phantom ship can follow us?"

O'Brien drew a long breath. "I don't have a clue as to how that ship—if it is a ship—is maintaining impulse speeds, let alone whether it's capable of warp."

"I'll bet we're going to find out," Sisko muttered. "But if they can make warp, running won't solve anything." He thumbed his chin as he gazed out the window, considering. "Let's try to outmaneuver them without leaving orbit."

"By keeping the planetoid between us and them?" O'Brien asked.

"Yes."

"I'm all for that."

"Good. Now let's take her down," Sisko said. "We'll skim the ionosphere just enough to create a charged particle trail. I want to compare our wake to theirs."

"Shields at maximum," O'Brien said. "Power optimal. This maneuver shouldn't be difficult. We could even duck into the atmosphere if we have to. Adjusting the shield geometry should only take a minute."

With a nod Sisko turned his attention to the controls and eased the runabout into a slow descent. Within seconds they had entered the thin wisps of hydrogen and ammonia that constituted the planetoid's upper atmosphere. He watched the monitors carefully, studying the result as heat from the friction of contact left a swirling blaze of color trailing the runabout in a slowly dissipating stream. Charged ion particles, excited by the runabout, left a clear sensor trail as well.

Sisko nudged the helm to port, then to starboard, then back again. He tensed as the second runabout followed along, shadowing them—but as it entered the atmosphere, almost no trail formed. Sensors showed almost no reaction of any kind. He frowned. A phantom ship indeed.

"They're matching us precisely," O'Brien said. "Speed, angle, pitch, and they're keeping exactly two hundred thousand kilometers between them and us."

"I'm going to go back to a higher orbit and cutting our speed," Sisko said, working the helm controls. He didn't feel like playing tag all day long. "Maybe it's time we tried to find out what they want." He waited until the *Rubicon* was again in a standard orbit, then cut their speed by half.

"The other ship is slowing down, matching orbits," O'Brien reported. He tried hailing them again, but as Sisko expected, the phantom runabout made no reply.

Sisko rubbed his jaw thoughtfully. He slowed again, letting their orbit slip once more, just a bit. And again the second runabout did the same. The two ships continued to track across the sky without incident for several minutes.

"At least they haven't powered up their weapons," O'Brien said. "None that we can read, anyway."

"Which is one reason why I'm beginning to wonder whether we should worry about them right now. They haven't done anything provocative, they won't answer our hails, they aren't attempting to communicate with us—hell, we don't even have a clue as to who or what they are. But they don't seem to pose any immediate threat, and we have a lot of work to do. I suggest we get to it."

"That simple, eh?" O'Brien said, adding a grin.

Sisko shrugged. "Maybe."

"I say they're not answering because there isn't anything there. Nothing real, I mean."

Sisko nodded. "Go back to scanning the planetoid. We'll just keep an eye on the runabout double for now."

O'Brien did as he was told. Sisko took the ship to an optimal sensor orbit, all the while continuing to observe their strange companion. In just a few minutes O'Brien started talking to himself.

"Would you like to share?" Sisko asked him, letting a look of amusement show.

"I would," O'Brien said. "Two things, as a matter of fact. But first I want to try changing course to a polar orbit, then coming back around in line with the equator."

"Very well." He made the course correction. "Why are we doing this?"

"If it's all the same, I'll let you know in a minute."

Sisko trusted O'Brien both as a friend and as an engineer—he had ever since the two had first gotten to know each other while turning a very Cardassian

Deep Space Nine into a station that they could live with. He knew how lucky he was to have gotten Miles O'Brien to leave the *U.S.S. Enterprise* and sign on with DS9. If O'Brien had a hunch, Sisko would indulge him.

They passed over the pole, then returned to their original orbit, picking up where they had left off.

"Strange," O'Brien said.

"You'd better say more than that, Chief."

O'Brien cleared his throat. "Sir, what we seem to have is exactly what it looks like—a miniature gas giant, which pretty much contradicts anything I know about cosmology. The planetoid's core is generating more heat than it should, given its mass. And then there's the atmosphere. A body that size can't generate a strong enough gravitational field to retain an atmosphere this dense. And I can't begin to explain all those plasma eddies we've been watching."

"So it might be worth sending a science team to investigate, after we get back to the station," Sisko said.

"Well, that's not all," O'Brien continued. "Those eddies are made up of some pretty intense electromagnetic fields. They seem to occur in a generally random pattern, which would indicate a natural condition, but there are repeated spikes, and the level and pattern of the spikes don't seem natural to me."

Sisko was listening intently now. "Explain."

"The more maneuvering we and that ghost ship do, the more the plasma activity within the sphere increases. The two seem to coincide precisely, and I've already ruled out sensor echo."

"Can we get a fix on the source of those spikes?"

"I've been trying," O'Brien said. "The source shifts randomly almost every time a surge falls off. I do have an approximate fix on something else, though. There's a growing source of concentrated low-band electrostatic activity, like a forcefield trying to organize. It's begun to show up on the thermal plane between the upper atmosphere and the first really dense layer of gas."

O'Brien seemed reluctant to jump to any conclusions, and Sisko felt the same way; certainly they had both run into stranger anomalies in this galaxy, and what they were picking up didn't necessarily have anything to do with Jake and Elliena. But at the moment they didn't have much else to go on, and Sisko had to be sure his son wasn't here before he could leave. "How big an area is involved?"

"The field is about one-point-three kilometers in diameter, but it's growing. I'm thinking that the runabout we have following us could be a projection of some kind, possibly originating from the energy wave source down there. But so far I haven't seen any evidence of projection devices or beamed particles."

"And none of that explains that phantom Klingon freighter."

"No, I don't suppose it does."

Sisko checked the results of their first full scan of the planetoid. There was no sign of the *Rio Grande*, and even if it had gone down here, there was almost no chance that anyone would still be alive on board, or that rescuers could reach them. It was the worst thought he'd had since arriving in the Gamma Quadrant. Quickly he pushed it away. Jake and Elliena couldn't be dead.

A more likely possibility was that they were adrift somewhere in the vast ocean of night or that they had been found and taken by whoever or whatever was responsible for these phantom spacecraft. Whether the planetoid or its anomalies had a connection to their disappearance or not, Sisko felt he wasn't getting any closer to the answers.

"Let's try another tack," he said. "I'm going to take her out of orbit. Then I'd like to pay our companions on the other runabout a visit."

"I'd advise against beaming over there," O'Brien said. "You're likely to beam yourself out into empty space."

Sisko grinned. "Thanks, Chief, but I wasn't planning on it."

Taking the controls once more, Sisko engaged the impulse engines, and the *Rubicon* broke out of orbit, then moved into open space. Just as expected, the second runabout followed.

"Reading, Chief?" Sisko asked, as he began to bring the *Rubicon* about to face their shadow.

"Nothing new."

"Ahead one-quarter impulse," he said as the distance between the twin ships began to diminish. "Let's get to know each other."

"How close are you trying to get?"

"Close enough to rub noses. Disarm the weapons and lower the shields, but be prepared to reactivate on my mark."

"We might be able to pass right through them," O'Brien speculated.

"I'm not going to try. I just want to provoke some kind of reaction."

"That's what I'm afraid of."

Sisko felt the silence in the runabout's control cabin pressing in on him as the two ships drew near each other. Just as they were about to touch, he cut power and thrustered the *Rubicon* to a full stop. The two ships hung nose to nose, only a few meters apart, while O'Brien continued scanning. Sisko could see now with his own eyes what the sensors were saying. He could make out the stars if he stared long enough into the image of the duplicate runabout.

O'Brien tried hailing one more time, but again there was no response. "Nothing," he said.

"We have to continue searching this sector," Sisko said, "but I have no doubt that our companion runabout will keep following us like a lost puppy, and I'm not having much luck getting used to that idea."

Sisko blinked as a proximity alarm began to chime from the main console. "Checking long-range sensors," O'Brien said, swiftly touching pads with his fingertips. He looked up at Sisko, eyes wide. "We've got another ship approaching at light-speed—no, make that two ships, and they both seem plenty real enough. Estimated speed warp eight-point-six."

"What's their heading?"

"They're on a direct course toward our position."

"Let's hope it's someone with some answers."

"I'm trying to get a positive . . ."

"What is it, Chief?"

"Captain, it might be prudent to back away from that other runabout and raise our shields, just in case. I recognize those warp signatures."

"Who are they?"

"Klingons."

CHAPTER 13

"DESTROYED?" KLARN SHOUTED. "All the crystals, *destroyed?* This had better be some kind of joke, Quark. Do you hear me? A bad joke, one that no one is laughing at!"

"It's no joke," Quark told DaiMon Klarn, whose glowering face continued to fill the main viewscreen in Ops. "But it wasn't my fault, I swear. It was the Aulep and the Rylep. They're crazy, always quarreling, shooting at each other, chasing each other around. They put pettiness ahead of profit. They're so . . . so unreliable." Quark leaned conspiratorially toward the screen and lowered his voice. "I can't be held responsible for their actions. The fact is, I was nearly killed in the attack that destroyed the crystals."

"It's a pity you weren't," Klarn said. "But I can

correct that oversight, Quark. It's also a pity you can't control your business partners, or choose them more wisely in the first place, but I can deal with them as well, if I must. You will tell me how you are going to replace that lost shipment or compensate me for my losses in full, plus a little extra for aggravation, preferably in gold-pressed latinum. And you will do it within one hour."

"But, Klarn, I can't possibly . . . I mean, you don't realize—"

"Someone had better make recompense. I do not care if it's you, the Aulep, the Rylep, the Beshiel, or the Bajoran Prophets!"

"Major, the Beshiel are targeting the Ferengi ship in direct response to DaiMon Klarn's threats," Worf said.

Kira stepped forward and took a sharp breath. "Listen to me, all of you. There will be no battle, I promise you that. The first ship that fires will be neutralized. I must assume you do not fully appreciate the extent of this station's firepower, but let me assure you that any hostile act will be short lived."

"I do not intend to fire on *Deep Space Nine* directly," Klarn insisted.

Kira spread her hands. "That doesn't matter. This is our space. Any weapons fire might result in damage to the station."

"The Federation would not risk firing first on a Ferengi vessel," Klarn countered coldly.

Kira smiled menacingly at him. "Perhaps not, but

a Bajoran major in Bajoran space just might. Now, Bedal, you will order your ships to power down their weapons. Klarn, you will do the same. After that, both of you are to come aboard the station so that we can attempt to work all of this out. Talks between Quark, the Aulep, and the Rylep have already begun, and you are welcome to join them—unarmed, of course. Meeting with us is your best option, Klarn. Your only other choice is to return home empty-handed or get blasted into whatever afterlife you believe in. You have five minutes to decide. Starting now." She turned to Dax and nodded, and the main screen went dark.

"You aren't really going to destroy them, are you?" Quark asked in earnest.

"It does seem prudent," Dorram said.

"I agree," said Flenn.

"I don't recall asking either one of you," Kira said, glaring. They averted their eyes. A tense silence followed. Kira stood, arms folded, waiting out the clock.

"Reopen all channels," she said, precisely at the five-minute mark. The screen came to life.

"We have considered your offer, Major," Bedal said before Kira could say a word. "It sounds reasonable enough."

"I fail to see what can be accomplished by talking," Klarn said.

"By attending the meeting you may be enlightened," Kira told him. "You have everything to gain and nothing to lose."

"I am losing valuable time."

"Then we'll try to keep the session brief," Kira said.

DaiMon Klarn made a face that Kira could only associate with acute indigestion. "Yes, yes, very well," he said, and the screen went dark.

"Major, Dr. Bashir would like to see you in the infirmary when you get a minute," Dax said, wincing in apparent sympathy.

Not another summons, Kira thought.

"Can it wait?"

"He says it should only take a moment."

"He always says it'll only take a moment," Kira said. "Monitor the new arrivals," she instructed Odo. "And post plenty of security. I'll be back shortly." She glanced at Dax again. "Tell the doctor I'll be right there, but I won't be smiling."

Dax grinned at her. "Yes, sir."

Dr. Bashir greeted Kira as she walked through the door. A look of mild exasperation tightened his fine features, but she already had a best guess as to what that was all about. It was the sort of look the doctor often wore when he had innocent casualties to tend to. In her estimation, he was still a bit too sensitive for a post like this, the sort of man who would have been more at home in an advanced treatment center somewhere on Earth or, better still, participating in a humanitarian aid mission to some plague-ravaged world. He was a gentle man, and *Deep Space Nine* had never been a gentle place.

But Bashir had asked to come here, to the frontier, and since arriving he had met the many challenges of that decision with courage, intelligence, and determination. Kira had come to respect him for all of that.

"I'm treating a couple from Bajor, and I thought you ought to talk to them," he said in a hushed voice.

"Why me?" There were other Bajorans on the station. She didn't think Bashir would call her here simply to offer comfort to some of her people.

"They were on their way to see Captain Sisko—something about a planetary resource project."

She still didn't see the urgency. "How badly were they injured?"

"Not too seriously. Their shuttle was damaged when that Klingon freighter exploded. But they've been asking to see their daughter. I thought I recognized their names, but I didn't realize until I checked that they're the parents of Tol Elliena"—Kira felt the weight of his words settle in her gut—"the girl who was on the *Rio Grande* with Jake," he finished. "I haven't told them, but I will if you want me to. The thing is, I don't know that much about what happened or about what's going on now."

"I don't know much more than you do." Kira sighed. "But you'll be happy to know I've persuaded a small fleet of Beshiel ships not to fire on us and convinced a Ferengi DaiMon not to fire on them— or on us. At least not for the moment. You might have been a lot busier in here."

"I do appreciate that, Major." Bashir smiled, letting her know he understood the strain she was under. "Tell you what," he added. "If you like, I'll talk to these two."

"No, I'll talk to them, but thanks for the offer."

"Has there been any word about Jake and Elliena?"

"No, not yet. The captain was scheduled to send a message buoy through the wormhole over an hour ago, but it hasn't shown up, and we haven't heard a thing from Jake. To tell you the truth I'm getting a little worried myself."

Bashir held her gaze for a moment, then turned in silence and led the way into the next room. Several other patients sat around. Only one seemed to be hurt seriously, a Starfleet yeoman lying on a biobed, apparently undergoing a scan. Two Bajorans, both in their forties, sat side by side on another bed. They wore well-tailored suits. The woman's was decorated with a subtle scrollwork pattern, and she clutched a fairly substantial matching shawl. Kira had seen Elliena only a few times, but the resemblance was clear.

"Major," Bashir said, indicating the two, "this is Tol Nareth and Tol Janin."

"The doctor tells us you have word of our daughter," Nareth said. Kira saw the concerned look of a parent strong in his eyes. His wife gasped a small breath. "We hated the idea of leaving her here, even for so short a time. It was irresponsible of us."

"I understand," Kira said, "but you mustn't

blame yourselves or second-guess your decisions. We all take our chances just getting out of bed in the morning, after all; both of you might just as easily have been killed in your shuttle when that freighter exploded, and Elliena along with you, if she'd been there."

"Why isn't she here?" Nareth said, rising, his expression changing to one of controlled distress.

"She was involved in that explosion, just as you were," Kira went on doggedly, "but the ship she was on was only slightly damaged."

Janin opened her mouth and brought her hand up to cover it as tears seeped from the corners of her eyes.

"What was my daughter doing on a ship?" Nareth demanded.

Kira paused, choosing her words, then forged ahead: "One of our officers was about to take her and Captain Sisko's son, Jake, on a brief tour of the solar system. Their runabout was thrown clear of the station and ended up entering the wormhole. We have every reason to believe they are all right. The captain himself has gone after them. He'll bring them back, I can promise you that."

Kira waited for the verbal explosion she was sure would come, but Elliena's parents only sat there, rigid with concern. When Janin found her voice she asked if there'd been any word.

"No, none yet, but I'm sure there will be any time now," Kira told them, with all the confidence she could muster.

"We've done this to her," Janin said, tears running down her cheeks now. "We never should have let her come here in the first place."

"No, no," Kira said, "you did nothing wrong. Just as no one here did. Any fault lies with those Klingon freighters."

"You've met the captain," Bashir offered, stepping forward. "He's the most capable man I know, and his son is a very resourceful young fellow. There's no reason to believe your daughter won't be back any time now, safe and sound."

Kira felt an urge to call Dax to see if a message buoy had come in since the last time she'd checked. But Dax would have called her if that had happened. "I assure you," Kira said, "we will let you know the minute we hear anything."

"And we will be here, waiting," Nareth said, though his tone carried more than a hint of accusation.

Kira and Bashir turned and left the room.

"We have to do something," Kira said as soon as they were alone. "I'm almost as concerned as they are."

"You aren't the only one who's worried, Major. This whole situation is driving everybody crazy. In the meantime, I'm about caught up here. Where are you headed now? I'd like to tag along."

"All right," Kira said softly. She headed straight for Ops with the doctor in tow. The moment they stepped off the lift, she called together the senior officers for an impromptu meeting.

"We should have had our second message from the captain by now, but there's been nothing," Dax said, when Kira and Dr. Bashir had briefed them on their meeting with Elliena's parents.

"It's not like Captain Sisko to miss a deadline," Odo said. "We have to consider the possibility that the Dominion has something to do with his silence."

Kira realized Odo had said this in part to spare anyone else from having to say it. Changelings, Odo's own people, were the Founders, the true power behind the Dominion. To his mind, though, with its keen sense of justice, the Founders represented a threat to peace, an evil he could not abide. Odo had wrestled with this paradox more than once, and his struggle always ended the same way.

"I propose we take the *Defiant* into the Gamma Quadrant to look for the runabouts," Worf said. "It has the cloaking device, the firepower, the speed, and the maneuverability needed to deal with whatever the captain and Jake may have encountered."

"We don't actually know that they've encountered anything," Bashir insisted.

"No, we don't, but Odo is right," Dax said. "There are any number of possibilities. And depending on how far the *Rio Grande* may have drifted, it could take a while to find them. It's also possible the captain sent a message, but the buoy was lost."

"Or he might be concerned that he's not the only one looking for the *Rio Grande*. A message buoy, if someone else found it, might put Jake and Elliena in greater jeopardy."

"Or the captain and Chief O'Brien have succeeded, and they're on their way back, which would put them here ahead of a buoy anyway," Kira said.

"Exactly," Bashir agreed, clearly trying to look hopeful. "It's easy to think the worst, but it isn't always necessary."

"I do not think we should leave their fate to chance," Worf said sharply, "or base our decisions on groundless speculation. We do not know where the second Klingon freighter went. We know only that something was there and that it had considerable firepower. We must also assume it followed the *Rio Grande* into the wormhole. The captain and Chief O'Brien cannot hope to combat such an adversary. However, the *Defiant* might. I would like to volunteer to lead that mission."

"I appreciate your concerns," Kira said. "I share all of them. And you're right, we can't wait much longer, and we need an advantage. But I'll take the *Defiant* myself, if and when it becomes necessary."

"Very well," Worf conceded cheerlessly. "Permission to serve as weapons and tactical officer."

"I'd like to grant your request, but I may need you here, Commander," Kira said.

Worf remained silent for a moment as he nodded, eyes averted, apparently thinking to himself. "Major," he said presently, "I was the one who suggested that Jake try full thrust in order to get free of the freighter's tractor beam. I feel . . . responsible."

"Don't blame yourself," Kira said. "Sisko gave the order. You only offered advice, and good advice at that. It got them loose, after all."

"Of course it did," Dax said. "What happened after that wasn't your fault."

"Even so," Worf said, "you may need my help in dealing with the Klingons, if you should encounter them."

"Point well taken," Kira said. "You're probably right. But nobody is going anywhere until we deal with the mess we've got right here. I can't run off on a rescue mission with several handfuls of visitors threatening to destroy one another and the station."

"Thank you, Major," Odo said. "I was beginning to think that all our diplomatic problems would be dumped in my lap."

"That won't happen just yet," Kira said. "But thanks for the suggestion." She sent the officers back to their stations. "Approximately how long since the second buoy was scheduled to reach us?" she asked Dax, once the lieutenant was in position.

"One hour, forty-three minutes."

"Very well. Send security around to the Aulep, the Rylep, the Beshiel, the Ferengi, and Quark. Explain nothing, but tell them to assemble in the meeting room."

"What if some of them refuse?" Dax asked, already starting to go about the task, but wearing a look of strained amusement on her face.

"I didn't say ask them, I said *tell* them," Kira said. She had no intention of letting them refuse.

"How do you plan to handle our esteemed guests this time?" Odo asked, lowering his voice to a confidential level. "I assume you have a plan."

Kira looked at him and sighed. "Yes, a plan. I just wish I knew what it was. . . ."

CHAPTER
14

"MINIMUM POWER HAS been restored," the computer reported, to Jake's considerable relief. The runabout's propulsion systems remained off-line, which meant he couldn't attempt to lift off right away, but at least the life-support system and some of the sensors now functioned.

"Looks like we might live a little while longer," he said, after he had explained the situation to Elliena. "Maybe we can even get an idea where we are and what happened."

Elliena sat patiently, though Jake noticed she kept tapping one foot nervously as he tried to scan their surroundings. He studied the sensor displays for several minutes.

"What's wrong?" she finally asked.

"I'm not reading any atmosphere at all out there,"

Jake said, worrying over the sensor panel controls. Had they malfunctioned? "This doesn't make any sense. It's as if we're still in space."

"But I can see atmosphere," Elliena said. Jake glanced through the window at the thick gray-and-white mist that swirled everywhere outside the runabout. "What I mean is, there's definitely something there."

"I know," Jake replied, turning with her. "And I know we landed on something solid. I felt it."

"So did I."

"So either we're both crazy, or we're having the same dream, or the sensors are wrong, because I'm not reading any surface, either."

"I'll pick that last one, but what do we do now?"

Jake considered his reply. Elliena was asking him straight out, as if she trusted him to know. That made him feel good, but the fact that he didn't have any answers made him more than a little uneasy. She seemed to sense this and looked away again, out the window.

"We could get out and take a look around," he suggested. "But without knowing what's out there, I think that would be too dangerous."

"As in, we could die instantly?"

"Well, yeah." Jake suddenly felt like an idiot. He glanced up and noticed that Elliena was grinning at him, if feebly, and he couldn't help grinning back. Which went a long way toward breaking the tension that had held half the breath in his lungs since the runabout stopped moving, and had nearly kept him from speaking for fear he would say the wrong thing. He kept thinking Elliena had to be even more concerned than he was; she wasn't used to any of this. He at least had been through a number of emergencies before. Yet she seemed to be managing her fears and was even able to kid with him just when he thought nothing would help ease her fears or his own.

"You're okay, you know that?" he said, though he found himself wishing he'd said it some other way even as he spoke.

"Thanks." She smiled again.

Jake felt a renewed sense of determination. "Okay, I'll tell you what I think. And maybe this time I'll get it right. Every time we've acted so far, it's resulted in a disaster. So I'd say the smartest thing we can do now is just sit tight for a while and wait. We know we were brought here deliberately. There has to be some reason. Someone is behind all this, and we should probably assume they're going to let us know what they want sooner or later."

"Do you really think so?" Elliena asked.

"Yes. If they wanted to destroy us they could have done that a couple of times by now. And something else: we're probably better off staying put than wandering around, because anyone from the station who comes looking for us will probably investigate this local phenomenon, whatever it is. They'll use a standard grid search pattern, which should locate the runabout, and us with it, if we're still here. If we were still drifting through space, we'd be harder to find."

"You're right."

Jake turned back to the instrument panels and studied the sensor displays. They flickered suddenly and began to change. He began to read an atmosphere, then gravity. Its sudden appearance didn't make much sense, but that was exactly what made the new information fit in with the rest of the data he'd observed: *nothing* here made sense. Yet the new readings gave him hope.

"What is it?" Elliena asked, apparently seeing his mood change.

"I don't know why, but I'm suddenly getting a lot of information. It looks as if there's a planet out there now, and we're on it. I don't think these mass and gravity readings could mean anything else. I'm even reading some kind of geologic formations; I just can't make any sense of them. What I don't understand is why we weren't getting these readings before or why the computer can't quite make sense of them. Insufficient data, I assume."

Jake looked at Elliena and shrugged.

"But you were right; we did land on something," Elliena said.

Jake nodded. "Or *in* something. We could have been pulled inside a ship of some kind. We could even be underground, for all I know. I don't think that would explain these physical readings, but I am picking up random energy discharges too—plasma spikes and surges that move in and out of sensor range like ghosts. They're not like anything I've seen around Bajor." He paused, letting his mind sort out the jumble of thoughts that clamored for attention or dismissal. "If we're aboard a ship, that might explain part of what's going on," he said more slowly. "These energy patterns aren't like the ones I remember from the station, either, but we might be dealing with an unknown alien technology." He stopped again and took a long, deep breath, then let it out slowly. The truth was, he just didn't know. "I'm starting to babble."

"I don't mind. Keep talking."

"The truth is, I haven't flown or trained enough to really know what's what. I'm not Chief O'Brien or my father. These energy spikes could be telling us everything we want to know, but I'm not getting it."

Elliena leaned closer to observe the displays. Jake let her see for herself. After a time she nodded. "Those readings remind me of the patterns of brain activity," she said.

"What made you think of that?" he asked. That comparison hadn't occurred to him, but he could see what she meant.

"I've been taking some premed courses. I'm thinking of going to a medical research school. Or I was, for a while."

"You never mentioned that before."

"I know. It's hard to choose your whole life when you haven't lived very much of it yet. There are a few other possibilities, some I've just thought of recently."

"Like what?"

"I'm thinking of maybe going into environmental research, like my parents. I know that's what they want me to do."

"But it's not what you want?" Jake asked, smiling at her.

"Well," she said, excitement creeping into her voice, "Bajor's full membership in the Federation could mean I'd stand a chance at getting into Starfleet Academy."

Jake sat back, eyes wide. "The *Academy?*"

"Sure. Why not? Is there anything wrong with wanting that?"

"No, of course not," Jake said, realizing how incredulous he'd sounded. He hoped she hadn't taken his surprise the wrong way.

"Or . . . or I don't know what else. The truth is, I'm not sure what I want to do."

Jake couldn't help but chuckle. He knew that feeling of uncertainty all too well.

"What?" Elliena asked.

"Me either. Maybe that's why I'm trying to be a writer. You can write and still do a lot of other stuff . . . anything, really."

"Really?"

"Yeah."

"I didn't realize," she said. She was looking at him with wide, intensely curious eyes. But he saw a touch of melancholy there as well.

"What's the matter?" he asked.

"I don't know. It's just that I thought for certain

you'd be going off to Starfleet Academy, and fairly soon. I keep picturing you exactly like your father, an officer, someday a captain. You're smart enough and brave enough."

She let her eyes wander off. Their relationship hadn't been very serious, he thought, or they had been trying to keep it from becoming that, Jake wasn't sure which. Both of them had known their time together would probably end when Elliena's parents left DS9. But he felt as if he could read her thoughts now. He felt exactly what she felt—he was sure of it. Caution wasn't the proper response anymore.

"Thank you," he said. "That means a lot."

"You're welcome." She winked. "Tell me, what does your father think?"

"Actually, Starfleet Academy is still what my father wants for me, but he's accepted the fact that it's not what I want. At least that's what he says."

Elliena tipped her head as if reconsidering him. "So, any idea what to do instead? While you work on writing, I mean."

"I've been accepted at the Pennington School in Wellington, New Zealand, back on Earth. A writing fellowship. I haven't decided if that's where I want to go yet. You have to get a lot of experience to be any good at writing. You have to live a lot and learn a lot. When my father and I took his light-sail ship to Cardassia, I told him I thought DS9 was a great place to get the experience I need. One of the best. He agreed."

"I read about that journey of yours. In fact, when I saw your picture, standing there with your father on that Bajoran light-sail ship after you arrived at Cardassia, I knew I had to meet you. It must have been wonderful."

"It was wonderful. I almost didn't go, but I'm glad I did."

A short silence passed. Elliena looked out the window once more at the swirling veil of mist. "I think maybe, if I do leave Bajor to study on some other world, I'll look back and say the same thing one day."

"Probably. I don't intend to stay on the station indefinitely. I'll probably go to Pennington eventually. Of course, there are other schools, other places. It's a big galaxy. I'm just a little too busy learning about the universe right here for the time being."

"That's pretty much the way I feel, but I've gotten to see only one small piece of one solar system. Of course, it is a very special piece. Bajor is my home, after all. But so is the rest of the galaxy, the way I see it."

Jake took both of her hands in his. "I know what you mean," he said. "And I think you're amazing."

She tipped her head. "I never dated a writer before."

"Oh, they are really special, no kidding."

"I don't doubt it."

He leaned over and kissed her, his hands gently tightening. When they parted, Jake felt a sudden twinge of doubt, as though he'd done something wrong. But as he let the look on her face guide his thinking, he was almost certain that he had done exactly the right thing at exactly the right time.

Elliena sat looking back at him, letting the softness in her eyes speak for her. He took a breath, then reminded himself that he had to keep trying to find a way out of the situation they were in. With a smile he let go of her hands and turned back to the sensor displays. Energy sources bolted this way and that, then trailed off, only to come back again—first one, then dozens, then a trailing pair.

"Computer, what is your analysis of the energy readings?"

"Energy patterns and intensity are not consistent with any known configuration," the computer voice responded.

Which was precisely what he expected.

"Is that why you wanted to spend time with me?" Elliena asked calmly.

Jake looked at her. "What do you mean?"

She smiled, but there was a hint of mischief in her eyes. "I mean, am I just another little adventure, a chance to learn something new to write about?"

"No," Jake said, trying to keep his expression dead serious, but her grin inspired him to return one of his own.

Elliena nodded. "It's actually true, isn't it, of both of us I mean; the adventure is what we're here for, at least to some extent. But I think that's okay."

"Good," Jake said, relieved that he had read her correctly. "But I think between us we've managed to find a little more adventure than we were hoping for." He gazed out the window again at the strange gray mist.

"I've heard that an adventure is something you only like to talk about once it's over," Elliena said.

"And how is that supposed to help us?"

"I don't have the slightest idea," she said, and she started to laugh.

Jake found himself moving to embrace her again. But just as they touched, someone—or something—started tapping on the runabout's hull.

CHAPTER
15

"WE'RE BEING SCANNED," O'Brien reported, concentrating on the display at his fingertips. "But I'm not sure by whom."

"It has to be the Klingons," Sisko said, half listening to the chief, half planning his next move as he watched the two Klingon vessels approach on the sensors.

"No, sir, it's not the Klingons, and it's not our runabout double, either. I'm trying to get a fix on the source."

"If the Klingons aren't scanning us yet, they soon will be; you can count on it." Sisko readied the warp drive. He didn't want to leave the area until he was satisfied Jake and Elliena weren't here, but he knew he might not have a choice.

"I've got a reading," O'Brien said, working at his

controls. "A very low energy sensor sweep is encompassing us and a good deal of open space around us. And it keeps moving. The beam may have found those Klingon ships by now—or it will any second. I can't say how long it's been there, maybe since we entered the area. We weren't scanning for anything this faint before."

"So where is it coming from?"

O'Brien concentrated for a moment, fingers once more playing piano on the panels before him; then he looked up sharply. "From the planetoid."

"But there's nothing down there. We just scanned most of the surface."

"Either we didn't see the source, or the scan comes and goes. Either way, there's something there now. And it's growing in intensity. The readings are in the same bandwidth as those we were picking up on the planet when we were in orbit, but they're much more organized and accurate. It's as if whoever is operating the beam knows exactly what he's looking for."

"Still no sign of the *Rio Grande*?" Sisko asked.

"No, sir."

Sisko glanced down at his own controls and turned his mind to the task at hand. The Klingons were dropping out of warp. The smaller of the two ships was a Bird-of-Prey, but the larger one was a Vor'cha-class attack cruiser, the Imperial fleet's largest and most powerful type of vessel, and there was no doubt as to their heading: straight toward the *Rubicon*.

"Keep the shields up, but don't target any of their weapons," Sisko said. "We don't want to start a fight we can't win. What do you say we greet our visitors?" He opened a channel and tried to introduce himself.

"I know who you are, Captain," said the Klingon who appeared on the *Rubicon*'s small viewscreen. "I am Drokas, commanding a task force charged with investigating the destruction of our freighter, the *Toknor*, at *Deep Space Nine*."

"In a way, we're here for the same reason. Perhaps we can help each other."

"You can help us and yourselves by—" Drokar stopped suddenly and turned his head, apparently listening to someone speaking to him from just beyond the view of the screen. When his eyes again met Sisko's, his look was far less cordial.

"Captain Sisko, I demand to be informed as to what kind of scan is being used on my ships. What is its purpose?"

"If you're referring to that soft energy scan emanating from the planetoid we just left, we don't know any more about it than you do," Sisko said with studied indifference. "I'm sure your own people have already told you the scan isn't coming from us."

"We are checking the origin of the scan at this very moment, Captain. Meanwhile," Drokas said, pausing as he adjusted his mass in his command chair, "perhaps you can enlighten me on another matter."

Sisko tried a tentative smile, for diplomacy's sake. "And what would that be?"

"I'm interested to know what new kind of shields the Federation is using, since we cannot get satisfactory readings on your other runabout. I would ask its pilot myself, but he will not answer our hails. It is some type of experimental craft, of course. Perhaps one that is experiencing . . . difficulties?"

"I'm sorry to disappoint you, Drokas, but that other runabout out there is not a Federation ship. We're getting the same readings—or lack of them. That vessel has been following us around like a lost dog. You're welcome to investigate, of course. And if you are able to tell us anything we don't know, we want to listen. In the meantime we'll do the same for you."

That seemed to slow the big Klingon's verbal charge, but Sisko knew he would recover quickly. He watched as Drokas turned away once more, speaking low, then nodded and spun back.

"Captain Sisko, we have verified the source of the scan to be a planetoid several million kilometers from here."

"About time," O'Brien said under his breath, though Drokas's scowl indicated he heard.

"That is consistent with our findings," Sisko said calmly.

"You will end the scan immediately!" Drokas said. "I am running short on patience, Captain. Obviously you are here testing secret weapons and technologies, and we have caught you at it. It is also clear to me that the *Toknor* must have stumbled onto one of your secrets when it passed this way—and you were willing to destroy our freighter in order to keep that secret. A base on that planetoid, perhaps? A Federation attempt to assert control over this entire sector?"

Sisko stared coldly at the Klingon captain. After a sufficient pause he leaned closer to the screen on the runabout's control panel. "Listen to me, Drokas. We've got nothing to do with that soft scan. We're being scanned, just as you are. And here's something else you should know: the *Toknor* was destroyed by an identical Klingon freighter, but we could get no firm readings of any kind from that ghost ship, just as we can get none from that other runabout out there."

"Silence!" Drokas shouted. "I have heard this story of Klingon attacking Klingon, of ghost ships disappearing. This is a Federation lie. I have no intention of believing anything so preposterous. But I will get at the truth, Captain, I assure you."

Drokas seemed to be a staunch, experienced warrior from the old school—a notably more popular faction in the Klingon Empire these days. He also seemed to be having a very bad day. Provoking him further would be counterproductive. But the truth had to count for something . . .

And that, Sisko began to realize, might be the very key he was looking for. Perhaps he couldn't dispel Drokar's federation fantasys, but if experience was any measure, he suspected that Drokas would soon have bigger problems to worry about—more than likely of his own making. While Klingons had many strengths, they could be intractable and slow to adapt, especially in confrontational situations. Sisko didn't know much about the phantom ships, but he knew exactly how they reacted to confrontations.

"Drokas, I'm telling you the truth," he began again. "If you don't believe me, I suggest you take one of your ships over to that other runabout and have a look for yourself. We have nothing to hide."

"We observed you in close proximity to the other runabout just before our arrival. You could have been setting some kind of trap. Our sensors do not tell us much. You might have taken the crew off the other runabout and arranged to destroy it and anyone who draws near it."

"Oh, brother," O'Brien muttered.

"You *are* a suspicious fellow, aren't you, Drokas?" Sisko said in spite of himself. He was at a disadvantage, no doubt of that, but there were limits to how much nonsense he could tolerate.

"You think me too suspicious, Captain, but I have survived a very long time that way. The very same way you have survived, I am sure."

"There is a difference between caution and paranoia, Drokas."

"And between heroes and fools." Drokas said. "I am no fool, Captain. I do not believe your stories, and I see no reason to trust you. I am being lied to by you just as I was lied to by that intractable Bajoran officer on *Deep Space Nine.*"

"Major Kira?" O'Brien whispered.

Sisko nodded. "I'm afraid so."

Drokas remained humorless. "I will not listen to this nonsense any longer. My mission here is clear. Yours is not. We are the ones with nothing to hide, not you. And we have lost a ship and a crew!"

"So have we," O'Brien snapped. "That's one of the reasons we're here."

"You say this only to trick me!" Drokas challenged, churning in his chair, as if the urge to leap up and physically engage his opponent might overwhelm him. Sisko repressed a wince as the leather segments in the Klingon's uniform made a chorus of ratcheting sounds.

"Drokas," Sisko said, "we have indeed lost a ship—a runabout—and a crew, but we don't think they were destroyed. They were catapulted into the wormhole when your freighter exploded. We are here to search for them and to gather information on the attack. Believe me, if there was anything we could have done to save your freighter or its crew, we would have."

"Preposterous!" Drokas said. "You say you search for a runabout, yet one lies astern of your vessel even as we speak. You cannot expect me to believe such nonsense!"

"That's *not* one of our ships!" O'Brien flared, finally agitated. "Don't you get it? That ship's some sort of projection. It's a reflection of this runabout, the same as the freighter that destroyed your freighter."

"Five minutes, Captain," Drokas came back, pounding his clenched fist on the arm of his command chair. "That is how long you have before I open fire."

The screen suddenly went dark.

"Well, what now?" O'Brien said, rolling his eyes. "Do we wait for the Cardassians to show up? Or maybe the Borg?"

Sisko knew the chief expected no answer. They couldn't seem to distance themselves from the ghost runabout, which continued to quietly match their every move, and they still had almost no idea who or what was behind the phantoms—or the anomalous planetoid they'd investigated. Sisko had hoped to entice Drokas into engaging the phantom, but that effort had failed as well.

Meanwhile their mission to find Jake and Elliena had been a complete failure so far, a situation that didn't seem likely to improve any time soon.

"The Klingons have got full weapons lock on us," O'Brien said.

"Let's try hailing Drokas again," Sisko said. "I have to find some way to reason with him."

"Good luck." O'Brien sighed, complying. "The channel is open, but they're not responding."

Sisko stared out the window. "Drokas, if you can hear me, I suggest that you scan the surface of that planetoid out there. It's true that the soft energy scans seem to be originating from there, but you won't find any evidence of Federation technologies or a Federation base. What you will find is that the surface is quite busy across a wide range of the electromagnetic spectrum. We haven't had time to analyze the data yet, but the activity may have something to do with these phantom ships. If you want, we'll lower our shields, and one of your men can beam over here here, while your other ship checks out the planetoid."

"I'm not sure I like the sound of that," O'Brien muttered.

"A reasonable suggestion, Captain, but as I said, you were here long before we arrived. Your people could have planted weapons on the surface of the planetoid, and you could raise your shields at least as quickly as we could fire our weapons, particularly if you know what is about to happen—and I do not. No, I will not bow to your suggestion; you will bow to my orders. Your time is up. I am giving you one last chance to comply."

"This is ridiculous, Drokas!" Sisko said, feeling the frustration now and beginning to lose his temper. "Attacking us won't solve your problems."

"I will be the judge of that," Drokas said. "Last chance."

Sisko glared at the Klingon. "But we don't have any information to give you!"

"A pity."

Again the screen went dark.

"The cruiser is powering up its forward disrupter," O'Brien said dully. "I don't think we're going to like this part."

"Shields at maximum," Sisko said.

"Already there," O'Brien answered. "Weapons armed," he added. "I'm locking on the cruiser first."

"We can't just sit here and be fired upon," Sisko said, taking the controls. "Let's try to move away, evade some of their fire, force them to shoot us in the back if they want to."

"Whatever you say, Captain," O'Brien replied soberly.

As Sisko brought the impulse engines into play, the runabout came around and began to move off.

"No good," O'Brien muttered. "I'm reading weapons discharge. They're firing."

Both men waited for the impact, but it didn't come.

"They're targeting the phantom runabout," O'Brien abruptly reported.

Sisko looked out the window to a clear view of both vessels. Disrupter fire blazed from the two Klingon ships, scoring direct hits, but their beams passed straight through the other runabout, as expected.

"Now maybe they'll believe us," Sisko said grimly.

O'Brien shook his head. "I doubt it. They're turning toward us now. They're firing!"

The *Rubicon* shook hard with the violence of the attack cruiser's massive disrupter assault. The cabin went dark as a shower of heat and sparks spewed from the main console. Sisko choked as smoke and the smell of burning metal and plastic filled his mouth and nose. Then the lights came back on as O'Brien worked to bypass overloaded systems.

"Shields down to thirty-one percent," the chief reported. "Another hit like that and we'll be in a lot of trouble."

"I know," Sisko said. "Coming about. Return fire!"

O'Brien complied. The cyclonic hiss of the *Rubicon*'s phasers filled the captain's ears.

"Direct hit, minimal effect," O'Brien stated.

"Target photon torpedo."

"Targeting. Ready."

But even as O'Brien spoke Drokas's ships fired again. The sound echoed through the hull with deafening volume this time. The runabout rocked violently once more, and the cabin was cast into darkness, replaced this time by the red wash of emergency lighting and fresh white-hot flashes bursting from the main and secondary consoles.

"That's done it," O'Brien said, already working to assess the damage. "The shields are down, along with half of our systems. I think we've still got the impulse engines, but I wouldn't count on it."

"I have to. We've got to try to dodge their fire."

Sisko stabbed at the engine controls. The runabout spun hard to starboard, forcing both officers to hang on to their seats despite the inertia dampeners. The attack cruiser's next shot went to the *Rubicon*'s port quarter, grazing the nacelles. The sound of the engines died, and the pull of the ship's sudden acceleration began to fade.

Sisko found his fingers tapping at dead panels.

"I'd say that was a low-energy precision shot,"

O'Brien went on. "Without our shields they could have destroyed us, but we're still here."

"The engines are gone," Sisko said in answer, giving up on the controls. For the moment at least, power wasn't coming back.

"Perhaps that's what they intended," O'Brien speculated. "Maybe they wanted to stop us but not kill us."

Sisko let a low groan leave his throat. "They've done that, but what I want to know is why."

"Captain, you'd better have a look at this." O'Brien pointed. The phantom runabout was still tagging along, but it had changed position and was turning toward the two Klingon battleships. It began to close the distance between them. Sisko watched closely as their look-alike drew to within point-blank range of the Klingons and opened fire, first on the Bird-of-Prey, then on the cruiser.

"Direct hit on Drokas's ship, heavy damage to their shields," O'Brien said, checking his sensor scans.

"The phantom is firing again," Sisko said.

"At the other ship this time—another direct hit."

The Klingons immediately fired back. Sisko watched as their disrupters lashed out once more, predictably passing straight through the phantom *Rubicon.* Twice more all three ships fired, sending streams of bright energy crisscrossing each other through the blackness of space.

Seconds later Sisko witnessed a series of violent

explosions. The Klingon Bird-of-Prey veered off the attack.

"Drokas's shields are down to twelve percent. The Bird-of-Prey has lost shields and taken heavy structural damage. They've still got partial impulse, at least for the moment."

"They've taken damage, all right." Sisko shook his head. "If the Klingons have any sense, they'll end this while they can still get away."

He stopped himself as he realize what the Bird-of-Prey was up to. He leaned forward, watching. "Looks like they're trying to circle around and catch the other runabout in a cross fire."

"I wouldn't recommend it," O'Brien remarked.

"Neither would I. Open a channel."

"Open, sir."

"Drokas, call off the attack! Your strategy isn't going to work. You can't damage that phantom ship, but it can destroy you. And if your firing patterns line up and your shots go through that ship, you could blow each other up. Either way, you're going to get yourselves killed."

"You will be dealt with before this is through!" Drokas shouted back, his signal coming in on audio only.

"More weapons fire," O'Brien said. Sisko looked up to see the Klingon cruiser closing in, beginning another attack. Slowly the phantom *Rubicon* turned directly into the Klingon's disrupter fire. Unharmed, it answered with a blinding energy beam of its own.

Without looking at the sensors, Sisko could see the increased intensity of the return fire. The phantom's beam struck the Bird-of-Prey amidships. The initial explosion seemed to break the Klingon ship nearly in half just before it erupted in a series of smaller explosions. A moment later nothing recognizable remained among the spreading debris cloud where the warship had been.

"Drokas has apparently ceased firing for now," O'Brien stated. "They're adjusting course away from us."

"Can't say that I blame them, but I doubt they're gone for good."

"Looks like they're going into warp," O'Brien said.

"What about our phantom friend?"

"Still sticking close to us."

"But I see nothing that would indicate any further hostile intent," Sisko mused, observing for himself. Then movement caught his eye . . . a large ship, coming from the region of space where the planetoid was located and traveling at near light-speed.

"I see it too," O'Brien said from beside him.

"What are you reading?"

"Nothing worth fussing over, same as the readings for our runabout friend, but this new ship is big."

"Big as a Klingon Vor'cha-class attack cruiser, I'd suspect," Sisko said as the second ghost ship passed by in full view, no more than a thousand kilometers from the *Rubicon*.

O'Brien checked his displays. "The new ship is

following Drokas's course exactly." He paused, then looked up. "They've just gone to warp."

"We have got to figure out who's controlling these ghost ships," Sisko said, feeling far more frustrated than he cared to admit.

"I'm with you, sir."

"Don't get me wrong," Sisko went on, "I don't mind that the Klingons are gone, and not a minute too soon, but everything we've seen proves that the intelligence behind these phantoms is highly advanced and not necessarily benevolent. We still don't know anything about them or what happened to Jake and Elliena, and we're no closer to getting the answers than we were when we left the station."

O'Brien said nothing, but the look in his eyes was one of empathy.

"Chief, send a message buoy back to the station letting them know what's happened. We're overdue as it is."

"Aye, sir," O'Brien replied. "What then?"

"We'll try to get these engines working. Then I wouldn't mind taking another look at that planetoid. For now it's all we've got, and I'm getting the feeling we've missed something bigger than that low-energy scan."

"No luck with the buoy, sir," O'Brien said, shaking his head. "The launch system is jammed. Probably damaged during the attack. I'd fix it, but I think we have higher priorities."

Sisko grimly nodded. Without a word he went back to work. O'Brien did the same. Within half an hour power levels were rising again and, with them, Sisko's mood.

"The repairs will take some time, but the damage wasn't as bad as I thought. We may even be able to restart the engines in a little while."

"Very good, Chief. Let's keep working."

"Captain, what do make of that?" O'Brien asked, glancing up at the sensor displays, where something had caught his eye.

As Sisko leaned over and examined the screen, his eyes went wide. A new atmosphere? How was this possible?

"Do a full scan, maximum range," he said.

"I'm recalibrating," O'Brien said, tapping at the console again, then waiting several seconds. New statistics on the planetoid appeared. "I'm reading an oxygen-nitrogen atmosphere on the surface. It's confined to an area only a few kilometers wide, but it's definitely there."

"Chief, wouldn't you say it corresponds pretty closely with the place where that soft-energy scan originated?"

O'Brien looked at him. "Almost precisely."

"How long before we can get under way?"

"We'll have maybe twenty-five percent impulse power in a few minutes, but it'll take a while to do any better than that."

"Let's hope that's enough to make orbit around the planetoid," Sisko said, preparing to take the helm once more. He almost grinned. It was the first time since arriving in the Gamma Quadrant that he'd felt as though something positive was happening.

"I don't think we have enough power to land or to use the transporters," O'Brien said.

"One step at a time, Chief," Sisko said, as he set a new course and watched the *Rubicon*'s engine balance. Slowly he began to accelerate. "What's our shadow up to?"

O'Brien checked. "The other runabout's still there. It'll probably follow us again."

"Good," Sisko said. "I'm starting to get used to it."

O'Brien frowned, incredulous. "That makes one of us," he said, as the engines shuddered back to life.

CHAPTER
16

"Sounds like we've got a visitor," Jake said.

"What kind of life-form could live out there?" Elliena wondered out loud.

Jake turned to stare at the rear of their compartment, toward the knocking they'd just heard. He'd counted a three-strike pattern, each rap loud enough to be the result of the hull being struck by a solid object at least as dense as hardwood.

Now only silence met his ears.

"Life seems to find a way of showing up almost everywhere in one form or another," Jake said. He turned back and hovered over the sensor displays. He recalled learning about certain gaseous entities, as well as ammonia-, sulfur-, and even silicate-based life-forms, but he didn't think many of those could wield heavy objects. He ran a broad scan, then ran it again and shook his head.

"What's wrong?" Elliena asked.

Jake tried to blink his bewilderment into submission. Courage aside, Elliena was counting on him to figure out what was going on and to decide what to do about it. He was the one with experience. Trouble was, he didn't have a clue.

"I'm not reading anything," he said. "Not even any wind, which is strange, because it was blowing at about twelve knots when we first arrived. My guess is there's ice of some type sailing around out there, and a wind gust carried a few chunks of it into our hull. That was the knocking we heard. Now the wind has died down, which means it shouldn't happen again."

That sounded good, he thought, even though he was just making it up. Ice would require frozen layers of gas or liquids, oceans perhaps, or precipitation, but he wasn't reading anything quite like that out there. It was possible that something was wrong with the sensors or that a localized anomaly was causing them to malfunction.

Thump.

"That sounded close to the bow," Elliena said. Jake followed her gaze. They couldn't see anything but the mist outside, but as Jake peered into it, he was almost certain that the gray-and-pink clouds swirling before him were getting thinner and visibility was increasing—although there still wasn't anything to actually look at.

Thump.

Thump.

"That was over here." Elliena gestured toward the ship's port side.

"You're right."

Jake ran another sensor sweep, convinced that it would do no good but desperate to do something. He came up empty again, except for a sharp rise in electromagnetic energy surges in the vicinity. Plasma currents ebbed and flowed all around the runabout. They seemed to swirl, blending and then separating, much like the mists they traveled through. But unlike the mists, the skittering energy fields were not dissipating.

"Do you still think those sounds are caused by ice chunks?" Elliena asked, clearly unconvinced.

"No, I don't. But I haven't got any other ideas. The impacts seem harmless enough, at least for now, but I wish I knew was causing them."

Thump.

Elliena nodded crisply. "Me too."

Suddenly the runabout moved.

Jake clung to his seat as the deck rose on the starboard side, high enough that Jake began to worry the ship might tip over and roll on its roof. He checked Elliena, found her hanging on, just as he was. Then they began to settle again, slowly, gently, until once more the runabout rested on level ground—or whatever it was resting on, since Jake still couldn't verify any true surface beneath them.

"I feel like a mouse being played with by a cat," Jake remarked. Elliena looked questioningly at him.

"Cats," Jake explained, "are small predators from Earth. People keep them as pets, but they retain most of their hunter instincts. They're cute. That is, a lot of people think they are. Mice are much smaller, like Bajoran lopets."

There were mice and even rats on DS9; they had followed humanity across the stars, just as they'd stowed away in past centuries on voyages across the seas of earth. And of course, several people on the station had cats. Jake didn't think Elliena had been on the station long enough to have come across any mice or rats, but the Bajoran equivalent, small, furry, tailless hoarders known as lopets were close enough, and a few had managed to find their way onto the station as well.

"But these cats don't eat their prey? They just play with it?"

"Usually. For a while, anyway. Cats have a sense of humor, you could say. Sometimes they'll bat the mouse around a little once they've gotten hold of it, to see if they can get it to run away again."

"They make a game of it?" Elliena asked.

"Yes, exactly. They're as playful as little kids—as long as they're not starving, that is. Still, nobody wants to be the mouse."

Elliena smiled despite this last grim reference to the two of them. "I would like to see one of these . . . cats someday."

"When we get back, I promise to show you one."

"Don't you mean *if* we get back?"

She was looking straight at him. It wasn't a fair question, but he couldn't fault her for forcing him to respond. "No," Jake said firmly. "When."

Thump.

Thump.

The runabout started rocking again, this time from side to side, though not so high as before and not so gently.

"Do you think they're trying to see if we'll run?" Elliena asked in a hushed voice.

"Or see if we'll do much of anything at all. Which is why I think we should do nothing. If we just play dead, whatever is out there might get bored and leave us alone after a while."

Elliena seemed to consider this a moment. "Does that work with cats?" she asked.

Not necessarily, Jake thought, but he told her, "Yes, most of the time." He just hoped whatever was out there wasn't hungry. . . .

With that the runabout jumped, then jolted forward several meters as if it had been kicked from behind. Then it stopped again, though smoothly, as though the hull had been sliding along for an instant on some type of ice. Nothing but silence followed. Jake still had ahold of his seat with a spasmed grip. He forced himself to loosen his fingers, then he realized he wasn't breathing and consciously drew a breath and let it out.

"Resistance," he mumbled, thinking out loud.

Elliena stared at him. "What?"

"Resistance. Friction. This is a level surface—at least right here it is. Whatever pushed us used considerable force, but we only slid a short way. We didn't keep going, which means that the surface we're resting on has got to be solid enough to create some drag. Rock or soil would have stopped us cold, but a compressed liquid or a frozen gas might cause us to."

"That's good, isn't it?"

"I think so. It means we probably won't sink. It also means that something pretty large could be walking around out there. Or a bunch of somethings."

He went back to the sensors and began scanning once more. The curious energy bursts were at a fever pitch now and seemed to be concentrated in the area immediately surrounding the runabout.

"Playing dead doesn't seem to be working," Elliena concluded.

Jake had been thinking the same thing. "Okay, maybe we should try doing the opposite. . . ."

Neither of them said anything for a moment. Action was the logical next step, but the possible outcome was far less certain. They'd had bad luck before, when they'd tried to get away from the phantom ship that had brought them here. Besides, Jake had no idea how to communicate with whatever was out there, or if communication was even possible. He had to consider the possibility that if he did the wrong thing, the consequences might be deadly.

"All right," Elliena said hesitantly. "What do you have in mind?"

"Something subtle. Something that won't use much power. We haven't got any to spare. But nothing that might be considered a hostile act. A benign signal of some kind."

"Why not flick the lights?"

Jake hadn't thought of that. The *Rio Grande* had numerous exterior lights, and he was guessing most of them were operational. In fact, he suddenly realized, those lights might be the very thing that had drawn attention to the ship.

On the other hand, they had been brought here deliberately; there was no question about that. So someone knew they were here. But Jake wasn't convinced that their abductors were responsible for what was happening now.

Whatever was thumping and jostling the runabout seemed curious, perhaps even playful, but it wasn't acting like the kind of alien who might be capable of the advanced technology and the violent attacks he had witnessed back at the station.

"Let's try it," he said. "Computer, darken all interior and exterior lighting for five seconds, then restore for another five seconds. Continue that pattern for thirty seconds."

"Is it okay if I'm a little bit scared?" Elliena asked.

She did not sound fearful, but she reached out and took Jake's hand again. He held it gently. "Yeah," he said. "Mind if I join you?"

She smiled weakly and squeezed.

Then the lights went out.

They came back on. Nothing had changed. They went out once more, then came on, repeating until the sequence ended. Still nothing. Jake found he'd been holding his breath.

"Maybe they can't see the lights?" Elliena suggested. "You know—no eyes, no faces."

That was entirely possible, given the environment. Vision in specific bandwidths was the sort of evolutionary trait that showed up only where it was needed. Jake glanced at the sensor displays once more, and his eyes went wide. He let go of Elliena's hand and leaned forward to hover directly over the console.

"What's wrong?"

"Nothing . . . exactly," Jake replied. "But something's going on out there. I'm reading an oxygen-nitrogen atmosphere now. It's all around us. Breathable air. And the outside temperature has gone up to twenty degrees Celsius. I'm getting more aggregate readings, too."

"The mist is still there," Elliena observed, "but it does look a lot thinner."

"And the colors are gone. It's all gray and white now."

"What do you suppose this means?"

"For one thing, it means we can probably get out and have a look around if we want to . . . if what we're seeing is real."

"Which could be a big 'if.' "

"I guess so."

"You think whoever is out there wants us to come out?"

"I think so," Jake replied. "Why else would they create a friendly environment around the runabout?"

Elliena nodded in agreement. They sat contemplating each other for a time, neither one speaking.

"Of course," Jake said, "that doesn't have to mean these life-forms are friendly."

"I knew that."

Jake shrugged. "We should wait awhile to see if the environment is going to go away. But if it doesn't, we'll have to step out sooner or later, and maybe we'll see who brought us here."

"Agreed."

Jake took a deep breath and sat back. "We'll give it ten minutes."

"Okay."

Jake didn't say anything else while the time passed, and neither did Elliena. After nine minutes and a few seconds Jake shook the tension out of his shoulders, then stood up. Elliena followed. She put a hand on his shoulder, and together they moved toward the hatch.

CHAPTER
17

"I THINK YOU'RE about to overload the universal translator," Odo said, leaning close to Major Kira's ear.

"I wouldn't be surprised," Dax said, overhearing.

Kira didn't say a thing. She was too busy keeping her eyes on all the participants. One by one, in the station's largest meeting room, they had gathered around the big table she had ordered set up. Kira sat at one end with Quark and Lieutenant Dax on her left, Bashir and Commander Worf on her right. Odo stood just behind her left shoulder, where he was simultaneously a comfort to her and a vexing presence to Quark. Odo seldom entered into diplomatic dealings, but in this instance Kira had encouraged him to put in a word if he felt so inclined.

The rest of the chairs, two on either side of the

table, were filled by the visiting commanders: Flenn of the Aulep, Dorram of the Rylep, Bedal of the Beshiel, and Klarn of the Ferengi. Of course they had begun arguing the moment they entered the room.

"This had better be brief and worth my while," Klarn said, finally addressing Kira. He had beamed aboard, having refused to dock his Marauder for "security" reasons. The others had made docking arrangements and come aboard, so Klarn's action had only added to the tension and soured everyone's mood, including Kira's, a bit further.

Kira sighed as Bedal leaped to his feet and shook a meaty fist at both Flenn and Dorram.

"We'd appreciate it if *everyone* could be seated now," Odo said firmly, placing a steady hand on the Beshiel's shoulder and gently pressing the commander back down into his chair. Bedal did not resist.

Flenn and Dorram rose in concert—a first, to Kira's eyes—to ward off Bedal's sudden bluster. But when Odo's security team moved toward them, they too settled back down.

For a brief moment this seemed to bring a relative quiet to the room, but in a few breaths the din rose again in earnest, rapidly becoming another shouting match. Kira looked to Klarn, who she noticed was uniquely silent. He appeared to be listening intently to the accusations and threats being bandied about. But even as she watched, she observed his mood turn from one of concentration to one of contempt. He leaned forward abruptly and slammed his fists onto the table, an action that once again brought an almost instant stillness. All eyes were on the Ferengi now.

"You people are pathetic," Klarn said, measuring every word. "There is no profit in arguing like children, and little hope that any of you will mature in the course of this meeting. You insist on behaving like fools. So I'll make this simple for you. I will be compensated in full for the crystals—equally by each of you, by tomorrow—or I will commence obliterating your ships one at a time until I get what I want. After that, your threats will not make a difference to anyone, especially me!"

"No one is going to obliterate anyone," Kira said sharply. "We've had too many threats and missteps already. We are here to find solutions to your problems, not to encourage discord. As a representative of Bajor I do not want a lot of new problems from the Gamma Quadrant spilling over into Bajoran space, and neither does the Federation. With the Dominion up to no good, we've already got our hands full."

"And I will not allow any of you to make this station your personal battleground," Odo added. "It is my job to keep the peace, and you can be certain that is exactly what I intend to do—whatever it takes."

"If I may," Dr. Bashir said, glancing at Kira. She

nodded for him to continue. "I would rather not have my infirmary piled high with casualties, and I don't think the rest of you really want that either. Surely you can resolve your differences without beating on one another or blowing each other up."

"No problem is without solutions," Dax said. Kira heard her speaking with the wisdom of a Trill's multiple lifetimes' experience, something she was glad for just now. Dax frowned at the meeting's attendee. "Is anyone here incapable of comprehending that idea?"

The combatants were looking at one another, their expressions twisting nervously. Kira nodded with satisfaction. When the question was put that way, it seemed, no one wanted to answer in the affirmative.

"I think Klarn had the right idea," Odo offered, moving back around the table and looking down his nose at the only other Ferengi present. "It seems to me that Quark is the one who ought to make things right among his associates, one way or another. After all, if it hadn't been for him, we wouldn't be having this discussion right now."

"I agree!" Klarn burst out.

Flenn, Dorram, and Bedal all chimed in, with considerable enthusiasm.

"Any response, Quark?" Kira asked.

Quark had that look again—the sort that usually proceeds from an intestinal blockage. "That suggestion is outrageous," he said anxiously, as though the ceiling might fall on him at any instant. "I can't afford to pay full compensation, even if you find some sort of twisted justification for it, which there isn't."

All four visitors broke into a fresh chorus off demands and accusations, though their words contained nothing that hadn't been said before. Kira, frowning, kept her attention on Quark. He was sitting there now, numbly listening to the torrent of abusive shouting directed at him. Though for all his melancholy, much of his trepidation seemed gone now, as if he had begun to grow weary.

"They're out for blood," Kira said. "Probably yours."

Quark nodded. "I know."

"If only it was that simple," Odo said.

"Agreed, but it's not, and this is getting us nowhere," Kira said, as Dax stood up and attempted to once again restore order. "I don't think these people are capable of reason," Kira said to Quark. "But perhaps you could come up with something that will suffice."

"You know, Major," Quark said evenly, "sometimes you get a question with no right answer."

Dax had the others somewhat subdued again. Kira turned to Worf, who had been completely silent so far.

"Holding back?" she asked.

"All three races are impossible to deal with," Worf said. "As far as I can determine, the Aulep, the Rylep, and the Ferengi are entirely without honor. I do not know how such races can survive. The Rylep and the Aulep especially. I have no sympathy for them, and while I will assist you any way I can, I have no wish to involve myself any more than necessary."

"Worf is just following my advice," Dax said. "I told him that it might be advisable for him to say as little as possible."

Worf made a growling sound somewhere deep in his throat.

Rom appeared in the doorway carrying a tray of drinks, giving everyone pause. He waited while the guards posted at the entrance stepped out of the way. Then he headed for the table and placed the visitors' drinks in front of them. Following Kira's lead, none of the station personnel had ordered anything.

"So, brother," Rom said, leaning close to one of Quark's great ears but speaking loudly enough. "I notice you can't find a way to make this deal work out."

"Your support is overwhelming," Quark grumbled.

Rom shook his head like a sculptor considering a ruined piece. "What's the matter?" he gloated. "You had plenty to say the other day."

"You live, you learn," Quark said. He sounded almost indignant, Kira thought. He waved Rom away. "Now go on. I have to think. Something you probably wouldn't understand."

Rom grinned as he moved on.

Kira stepped forward and clapped sharply to get everyone's attention. "The reality you each seem reluctant to face is that without any merchandise, the deal that brought all of you here is extinct. And while there is plenty of blame to go around, and plenty of deserving shoulders to rest it on, no one person deserves it all. You threaten one another, but you must admit that none of you stands to gain from attempting to annihilate the other."

"There is everything to gain from the destruction or, at the very least, the prompt imprisonment of these Aulep pirates," Dorram declared. "And my people are not alone in that opinion."

"I challenge you to cite one single creature in all the cosmos who would mourn your passing!" Flenn responded.

"The Aulep and the Rylep are festering lesions that should be removed from the face of the universe!" Bedal said. "They will stop at nothing, even going so far as to build Beshiel look-alike ships to trick us, so they can ravage our colonies and pillage our trade routes!"

"It is the Rylep who have done all this and more to us," Flenn said. "They have tried to fool us with an exotic new vessel that we take to be our own, until it is too late."

"More lies!" Dorram roared. "The Aulep constructed a highly advanced mock Rylep cruiser capable of destroying our ships with complete impunity—proof that nothing is beneath them and that they are becoming much too dangerous!"

Klarn and leaned over the table, wide nostrils flaring. "I would be happy to destroy any and all of you, any ship that looked as if it belonged to any of you, and perhaps Quark in the bargain, on behalf of any party who chooses to compensate me in full for my losses, which now include this colossal waste of time!"

"They sounded like they're talking about the freighter that attacked the *Toknor*," Worf said, heedful.

Dax nodded. "I was just thinking the same thing."

"Gentlemen," Kira said, acknowledging both officers, then turning to the others. "I suspect that there is some connection between all these look-alike ships firing on one another."

"Of course—the Rylep and the Aulep are coconspirators!" said Bedal.

"You mean the Beshiel and the Aulep!" Dorram said.

"I say the conspirators are the Beshiel and the Rylep!" Flenn answered them.

"I knew he would say that," Worf said, frowning.

"We're still not getting anywhere," Dax said, shaking her head wearily.

"The situation does look a bit hopeless," Kira accorded her.

"Maybe not," said Quark.

Kira turned and looked at him. "It's not?"

Quark held her gaze for a moment, and she saw intense concentration in his eyes. He looked almost frightening—like someone preparing to justify his behavior to his maker, though she saw something that reminded her of a cornered predator as well.

Quark slowly turned to the others seated at the

table, who were avidly continuing their arguments, and his expression began to change. He began using his stubby fingers as if to categorize whatever he was thinking about.

Kira looked on with mounting curiosity. "What is it, Quark?" she asked. "What are you up to?"

Quark swallowed hard. "Major, I think I've found a way out of this."

"This I have to hear," Odo said politely.

"I'm listening," Kira told Quark.

"Maybe I should just begin," Quark said hoarsely. He put his hand on Kira's forearm. She had an urge to pull away, but did not. "It would take too long to explain," he added.

"Try me," Kira said.

Quark's eyes narrowed. "No," he said. "We don't have a lot of time. Just listen to them."

"Thieves!" Dorram was shouting.

"Parasites!" Flenn countered.

"Barbarians!" Bedal told them both.

"Worthless fools!" Klarn told the entire room.

"Bodies will soon be piling up all over this station," Quark continued in earnest, "and one of them might be mine. Major, please, just follow my lead."

She leaned toward him. "Quark, you've got to be kidding."

"I've never been more serious in my life. Do as I ask, just this once. Trust me."

Kira's eyebrows went all the way up. "Trust . . . *you?*"

"I don't want to get in the middle of this," Dr.

Bashir said, his first words in several minutes, "but at this point I'd say that even playing along with Quark probably can't hurt."

Quark made a face that somehow managed to mix chagrin and distress in equal parts.

Kira shrugged. She might as well give it a try. "They're all yours, Quark."

Slowly Quark stood up, then waved stubby fingers through the air. "Gentle-beings, may I have your attention?"

He did not get their attention. He drew a deep breath, furrowed his brow, slapped his hands down on the table Klarn-like, and yelled: "Shut up and listen! All of you!"

This seemed to have the desired effect, Kira thought.

"Now, what we have here is a case of extreme shortsightedness, which has left all of you blind to the considerable assets, resources, and opportunities available here. You're all so busy worrying about the mistakes of the past that you're ignoring the future."

"Get to the point, Quark," Klarn said. "That is, if you have one."

"I intend to," Quark replied, beginning to show his form, flashing DaiMon Klarn an impish, almost condescending smile. Kira watched with increasing amazement. Quark clearly had hold of something solid, and he wasn't about to let go.

"For starters," Quark said, "I'd like to ask the Beshiel what they have been doing, and what they intend to do in the future, with the all of the riches they now mine?"

"We sell them, of course," Bedal said. "We've had trade agreements with two neighboring star systems for many years, and we have been negotiating with another, but we have to contend with constant raids, which disrupt our deliveries."

Quark nodded. "So you have only two customers now?"

Bedal glanced briefly about before saying, "Yes."

"But I'd bet your production capabilities are much greater than that."

"They . . . might be," Bedal said, clearly growing suspicious.

"Well, you see, you need new customers!" Quark grinned only slightly as he leaned toward Klarn. "And those customers should be the Ferengi!"

The combatants exchanged glances, but for a tense moment no one said a word. Klarn opened his mouth to speak.

"Instead of a onetime deal, the Ferengi can buy regular shipments," Quark went on, interrupting Klarn with perfect timing. "And not just of one kind of crystal, either. You'll also have the Federation as a customer if you do this right. Possibly Bajor as well. Best of all, their ships will come to you. The Dominion is a real threat, but the Ferengi have been conducting trade in the Gamma Quadrant for some time now, and the Jem'Hadar have left them alone. The Federation, of course, can take care of itself. As for other local threats, I'd be willing to bet that there aren't many races in your part of the galaxy that would be foolish enough to attack Federation or Ferengi vessels in open space."

"No one with any sense," Worf said.

"I'd say that's a fair statement," Kira said. She looked at Flenn, then at Klarn, following Quark's sharp gaze.

"What do you say to that, Klarn?" Quark asked the brooding DaiMon.

Klarn seemed to grow more reflective. "I say . . . let anyone try to stop one of our ships from taking delivery."

"Perhaps even the Klingons would be interested in a trade agreement," Quark added, looking to Worf. "I certainly don't think anyone is eager to attack them."

Worf shot back a look of collusion, then paused before answering. "I can not speak for my people, but they are clearly attempting to establish themselves on both sides of the wormhole. Trade is already a part of that effort. And I'm sure they would . . . welcome, equally, any attempt to assist or to stop them."

"Of course!" Quark added, turning to Kira, his expression conveying an urgent appeal for continued support. "Major, tell them about Bajor."

"Yes," Kira said, amazed and catching up. "Yes, I'm certain Bajor and the Federation would be pleased to open trade with the Beshiel and perhaps to offer short-term assistance, should any be required. Along with currency, I'd say that technologies can be exchanged as well. With time, the Beshiel might be able to upgrade their fleet so that the threat from interlopers would be lessened."

"We might also be able to offer medical assistance," Bashir offered, "in return for . . ." He paused, clearly at a loss. "For whatever it is we'll want."

Kira turned toward Dorram. He seemed to find the tabletop quite interesting just then. When no one said anything else, he cleared his throat. "But what of us?" he asked, though not of anyone in particular. "How does all of this benefit the Rylep?"

"Or the Aulep?" Flenn said, his voice hardening.

"What about that, Quark?" Dax asked.

"It's a big quadrant," Quark scoffed. "If I know Aulep and the Rylep, it won't take them long to think of something."

Odo looked at Flenn and Dorram. "For the time being," he said, "I would advise you two to consider another line of work."

Bedal seemed quite pleased with everything he was hearing, but now he turned to Odo. "Constable," he said, "it is no doubt a sad thing, but I do not believe that Flenn and Dorram know how to do anything else. They have always been thieves."

"Perhaps that's true," Kira said, getting everyone's attention as she sorted through thoughts that were still coming to her. "But they do know their way around your sector of the Gamma Quadrant. And there must be many other races on other worlds, many buyers, even sellers, waiting to be found. You'll all have to go a little farther, work a little harder, but it seems to me that Flenn and Dorram could do what Quark does: broker deals for the Beshiel and for whoever else is involved—for a reasonable percentage of the profit, of course. In fact," she added, leaning toward Quark and lightly stroking one of his very large and sensitive ears to ensure his compliance, "I'll bet that's just what Quark was about to say."

Quark looked strained, but then his face softened and his eyes grew keen. "Actually, Major, that's not a bad idea."

"I know."

"But there are so many possible trading partners," Klarn said, clearly restless. "Major, surely you'd agree that too much competition is not a good thing."

Kira grinned at him. "Um, no, I would not agree with that at all."

Quark turned to Klarn and shook his head. "Forget it," he said. "She's hopeless."

Kira found Flenn and Dorram huddled together over their end of the table, mumbling away and nodding with reserved but apparently genuine agreement about something. Kira didn't care what that was all about; she just took it as a very good sign.

"The entire arrangement sounds quite marvelous," Dax said. "Both Quark and Major Kira should be commended."

"I agree," Bashir chimed in.

Kira sat back and breathed an enormous sigh. "Very well," she said. "Why don't we take a break, get everyone settled in, then start working out all the details. DaiMon Klarn, maybe we could even get that Marauder of yours docked."

"I . . . think we can do that," Klarn said cautiously.

"Excellent." Kira stood up. "Dax?"

"I'll see to it," she said.

The mood remained hopeful as everyone rose. Kira decided she hadn't felt this relieved in months.

"You know, Quark," Odo said, coming around the table and putting one hand on the Ferengi's shoulder. "Sometimes you surprise me."

"I was about to say the same thing," Kira said.

"Well, it's about time someone said something nice to me," Quark replied. "I've never claimed to know everything, but once in a while I outdo myself."

"In a manner of speaking," Odo muttered.

Quark ignored him. "These sorts of negotiations are kind of exciting, when you think about it, even when you think you might lose. But that's what I like about gambling. It's exactly like life, a great and complicated game. You learn something new every day, but you can never foresee the outcome."

"Unless you cheat," Odo said.

225

"Thanks for pointing that out," said Quark.

"Why, you're welcome," Odo said with flair.

"You can all be as smug as you like," Quark replied, "but has anyone noticed that I'm the only one who came up empty-handed in all of this?"

"Oh, I don't know," Kira cooed softly, "you have our undying gratitude."

Odo grinned sharply at Quark. "Well, you have Kira's, at least."

Quark shook his head and headed toward the corridor.

"Getting back to the Gamma Quadrant," Kira said, turning to the others. "I think things here will be calm for a day or so. Meanwhile, we've got some people missing."

"I was wondering when you'd get back to that," Bashir said.

"The *Defiant* is on standby," Worf reported.

That was exactly what Kira had wanted to hear. But she had changed her mind about the command of the search mission. Sisko had left her in charge of the station; this was Bajoran space, and Kira had been dealing with the people in this sector and serving as first officer on *Deep Space Nine* for a long time. And although Worf outranked her, he had never challenged her authority here. But aboard a starship traveling into the unknown, Worf was clearly the veteran, and he had made the *Defiant* his personal pastime, had even moved into one of its crew quarters. Kira had no reservations about deferring to him now.

"Commander," she said, standing straight before him, "You will command this mission."

Worf looked at her with solemn eyes and nodded once. "Acknowledged," he said simply. He turned to address the others present. "We will assemble aboard the *Defiant* in thirty minutes," he said. Then he headed out of the room.

CHAPTER
18

O'BRIEN WATCHED SISKO play his fingers over the runabout's helm controls, only to wind up shaking his head in frustration. The news wasn't good.

"We'll be lucky if we make orbit," O'Brien said cheerlessly. "We have enough power, the planetoid's gravity isn't strong, and I can't see anything wrong with the controls, but somehow we're not making the trajectory."

He'd tried every available bypass and auxiliary system; he'd even attempted to patch impulse power through one of the warp nacelle EPS power feeds, but none of his efforts had done the trick. Available impulse power had reached what should have been a sufficient level to push them into a high orbit and keep them there, but that just wasn't happening.

"Our course is much too steep, that's certain,"

Sisko said as he continued working the controls, trying to correct the runabout's course. The tension was clear on his face, something O'Brien didn't get a chance to see very often. The captain was as cool as they came—too cool at times, according to some—but that suited O'Brien well enough. He didn't like commanders who overreacted and fussed all the time, the kind who got so involved in other people's jobs that they wound up making those jobs impossible to accomplish. Benjamin Sisko had the ability to recognize competence and act accordingly. The catch was that you had to live up to his expectations. When he needed you to come up with results, you just didn't let him down. And now, letting the captain down was exactly what O'Brien felt he was doing.

"What are the chances that we'll burn up?" Sisko asked, though O'Brien thought he'd guessed the answer already.

"It's a possibility," the chief admitted. "Too soon to say for sure. As long as we maintain control we stand a better than even chance. From what I read of that atmosphere, it's pretty thin. We should be able to fly around in there, at least for a while."

Sisko looked at him. "But?"

"I wouldn't count on it. I mean, we should be able to change course, too, but we can't."

"Then we'll just keep working at it."

Sisko sat back suddenly and let his hands hang in the air before him, and O'Brien thought he might be about to pound both of them on the runabout's console. Instead he pressed his palms together, prayerlike, deep in thought. "It's as if something is pulling at us just hard enough to prevent whatever we try to do, thwarting our efforts each time we make a move," he said.

"I'm still scanning for tractor beams or forcefields, but I'm not picking anything up—at least not in proximity to us," O'Brien said. "I'm just reading that low-frequency scan, same as before."

"I know, but everything we've seen so far has been barely detectable on our sensors—the other Klingon freighter, the other runabout—yet they seem to have had more than enough power and substance to destroy anyone who engaged them. At such faint levels it's almost impossible to analyze a scan correctly, even in open space; that planetoid is still emitting enough random energy to scramble any normal signal."

"Aye," O'Brien said simply. The captain knew almost as much about science and engineering as his science and engineering officers. That was something else O'Brien admired about him. That and the fact that Sisko didn't use his own expertise as a wedge between himself and his people.

O'Brien tried one last revised subroutine designed to circumvent the impulse engine's balance limitations. The result was minimal.

"Sorry," O'Brien said, looking up from his consoles, shaking his head slowly. "That's all you're going to get out of her for now. I don't think it'll be enough."

"Even though it should be."

O'Brien shrugged. "Nothing lately has been what it should be."

O'Brien watched the planetoid grow large in the windows again, its swirling gases spinning in dull shades of orange, pink, and white. "There must be something there," he said.

"I've got a feeling we're about to find out, one way or the other." Sisko went back to hovering over the helm controls as if willing them to do his bidding. O'Brien had seen that technique work more than once.

Another few moments passed as visible wisps of atmosphere began to slither past the windows, signaling the beginning of their descent. "Coming up on entry," he said. "We should start getting a bit warm."

"Maybe not, Chief. The helm is responding a little better. I'm getting latitude control back."

O'Brien peered at his consoles, surprised. "I'm reading increased power flow."

"It might just be enough to pull us out of this dive and into a low orbit."

"I think you're right," O'Brien said, attempting to verify. "But don't ask me to explain what the hell is going on."

The runabout rattled and shook for several seconds, and O'Brien felt his insides swirl. Then the ride became smooth. He heard Sisko exhale with relief as the planet stopped charging up toward them and began instead to turn beneath them.

"We won't be able to maintain such a low orbit for long," O'Brien reported. "Still, it might give me time to get the engines working well enough to get us out of here."

"I don't know about that, Chief. We may not be leaving just yet."

O'Brien looked up, saw the captain intent on his instruments again. "Why not?"

"What do you make of this?" Sisko asked, pointing to a sensor display. O'Brien's eyes opened wide as he ran a quick check of his own. The anomaly he was reading on the planet below covered an area several dozen meters across, an islandlike bubble containing an oxygen-nitrogen atmosphere and displaying consistent coordinates. A remarkably stable area, O'Brien decided, as he continued to analyze the readings.

"I don't know," O'Brien said, "but it shouldn't be there."

"We're losing altitude again," Sisko said flatly.

Once more O'Brien turned his attention to the flight stats. It was true. They were going down, and quickly. "This just doesn't make sense!" O'Brien said, his Irish brogue getting noticeably thicker as his frustration increased.

"Well, it's nice to know this can't be happening," Sisko said, shaking his head. "So how about fixing it?"

"Yes sir," O'Brien said, somewhat chagrined. He started running systems checks again, the same ones he had just run through only a few minutes ago. This planet seemed determined to see the *Rubicon* destroyed in a fiery, falling blaze, no matter what he tried to do to stop it, but that didn't mean he could lessen his efforts. There had to be an answer.

"I'm picking something up now," Sisko said. "There."

O'Brien followed the captain's finger to one of the sensor displays. What he saw reminded him of a small beacon, a thin beam of energy no more intense than that of a handheld flashlight, but more concentrated than anything they'd detected so far. It was emanating from the atmospheric bubble on the planetoid below, and its target was clearly the *Rubicon*. The chief wasn't sure whether the beam had just been activated or whether their proximity to its source had made it more easily detectable.

"Looks like we're being guided down," he said.

"It does at that," Sisko said. "I just hope they know what they're doing."

"If they don't, there isn't going to be much left of us once we finally do arrive."

The runabout surged, then slowed and adjusted its trajectory to the proper angle of descent, more or less. Control was beginning to return yet again. Sisko worked, with no success, to correct their flight path.

"I'd say we're supposed to head for that bubble of atmosphere," O'Brien said, pointing.

"It looks that way. What do the scans show now?"

"A hotbed of electromagnetic plasma currents. Other than that, nothing has changed."

"Have you noticed that our little look-alike runabout has stopped tailing us?"

In truth, O'Brien had nearly forgotten about it. "I guess I haven't," he said.

"You've been a bit busy, Chief. That's why I pointed it out. I get the feeling that everything here is being orchestrated by someone, probably on the planetoid itself, someone who's using it as a base, perhaps. And I wouldn't be surprised if what's happening to us isn't exactly what happened to Jake and Elliena. That might explain why we haven't seen a trace of them anywhere."

"We're nearing the surface," O'Brien said, tapping at the sensor panel. "Or what I think is a surface, although we're not picking up anything solid. Not yet, anyway. The interference is pretty bad."

"I'm going to try bringing her in."

"Right." O'Brien watched every system, looking for any bit of energy or control he could give the captain.

"You've got thrusters," he told Sisko a moment later, and he watched the captain fire them almost instantly. The *Rubicon* bobbed gently, then leveled out, drifting through a thick yellow cloud. It slid into a lighter field of swirling haze, then down again until it finally came to rest. Outside, through the windows, O'Brien saw a twilight world of changing gray-and-white mist.

He glanced at Sisko. "Now what?"

Sisko took a deep breath, then huffed it out. "Unless we can think of a reason not to, I don't think we have any choice but to get out and have a look around. According to our sensors, the atmosphere is breathable. Bring a tricorder. I'm going to want continuous scans."

"Right behind you."

They made their way to the hatch, opened it, and stepped out onto the alien surface—a dark material that resembled pavement, though it was a little smoother and, as O'Brien discovered when he bent over to touch the ground, slightly warm. He sniffed cautiously. The air had no odor at all, but it was moist, warm, and pleasant—except for the mist, which reduced visibility to only a few meters.

"We'll walk circles clockwise around the runabout, then widen our course each time around," Sisko said. "Keep scanning. Maybe we'll run into something."

"We could walk right into each other in this soup," O'Brien grumbled, though he was already moving. They walked slowly, minding the extent of their visual range so as not to step off any cliffs or into any holes. After the fifth circle, which was wide enough for them to lose sight of the runabout completely, they found no irregularities on the surface or in the mist. In fact, they found nothing at all.

"It's as if we're being stored here for safekeeping," O'Brien finally said.

"But for what purpose?"

"I kind of hate to think about it."

O'Brien jumped as his tricorder chirped. He looked down to find the EM levels leaping up the scale from a point just a few meters away. "Energy contact," he stated. "Dead ahead."

"Source?"

"Unknown. It's just . . . there. But it could have come from anywhere around us. I don't think it's a weapon, but there's no way to be sure."

Sisko drew his phaser. O'Brien followed.

"I'd rather not shoot first," Sisko said. "We don't want anyone getting trigger-happy with us."

O'Brien suddenly drew a breath. "Captain, I'm reading two distinct contacts now, side by side, both faint but steady. They've started moving." He looked up from his tricorder. "Straight this way."

"Phasers on stun. We'll stand our ground, but that's all we'll do until we figure this thing out."

O'Brien peered into the thick, swirling air before him. "Whatever they are, we should be able to see them right about now." He squinted, blinked, then . . .

"I see them, Captain, there." He pointed, and Sisko's eyes followed as two humanoid figures emerged from the mist and walked steadily closer. They were wearing Starfleet uniforms—or what resembled uniforms. And as they drew closer, other specifics emerged. The devil was in the details, but the chief recognized the taller, dark-skinned man on the right and the slightly shorter, lighter-complexioned fellow who strode along beside the first: Captain Benjamin Sisko and Chief Miles O'Brien.

CHAPTER
19

JAKE STOOD CLOSE to Elliena, furtively peering into the swirling gray-white wash that filled the air around them. He felt inert, as though the universe had ceased to exist as he had known it and had shifted into some other, transitional dimension. He glanced back at the *Rio Grande,* a reassuring symbol of reality, the only one, aside from Elliena. A chill tingled his spine; he tried to attribute it to the dampness that made his clothing feel limp and heavy and made his face and hands moist to the touch. He drew a deep, calming breath and noticed that the air had no scent to it at all.

"Do you feel strange?" Elliena asked, her gentle voice just above a whisper.

"What kind of strange?"

"As if someone's watching us?"

Jake considered this and realized she had identified part of the uneasiness he felt. But it was more than that: he felt as if they were being probed. "You'd think we would have been contacted by now."

"What's that?" Elliena said, pointing ahead and to the left. Jake peered into the mist and saw that something was taking shape—silhouettes emerging slowly, growing larger.

"Cardassians!" Elliena shrieked. She grabbed Jake's arm and tried to pull him toward the runabout. He blinked twice and decided she was right, as he began to distinguish the ridges on their faces, the thick neck arteries that fanned out on either side of their heads and smoothed into their shoulders. Five figures in all, each one armed with energy rifles and dressed in standard Cardassian military uniforms, all of them taking aim at Jake and Elliena. The Cardassians began to fan out, flanking their prey.

"We're not at war with Cardassia," Jake pointed out.

"Then why are they doing this to us?"

"I was wondering the same thing," Jake said. "Let's play it safe. Back up slowly. They could have gunned us down already if they'd wanted to, so maybe they want us alive."

"Back up where?" Elliena asked, already taking step back with Jake, reaching out to touch his arm for guidance.

"The runabout's hatch is still open. We might have time to get through it before they can stop us."

"And what then?"

Jake saw the fear in her eyes, deeper, more intense than anything he had seen there before, despite all they had been through. The legacy of Cardassia's occupation of Bajor had done this to her. Jake had come to know enough Bajorans to understand what it meant to endure that kind of suffering, to live in that shadow.

Major Kira had fought the Cardassians ever since she was a child, but she had learned to deal with Gul DuKat and numerous other Cardassian officers since being posted to *Deep Space Nine*. She even got along with Garak, the station's only resident Cardassian, who in turn seemed to get along well enough with her.

But for Elliena it was different. Jake knew enough earth history to draw a quick comparison. He knew what hate groups like the Nazis had done to Jews and others during the 1940s, what white supremacists had done to his own black ancestors in the southern United States and in Africa during past centuries—and these were just two examples of the long, puzzling saga of man's inhumanity to man. But Elliena had lived more than half her life under Cardassian occupation, and the rest of her knowledge had come from firsthand accounts, stories, books, and recorded images, all filled with the graphic reports of what Cardassians had done to her people and her planet. Now, before her eyes, all of that torment had come walking out of the mist in the form of five specters from a living nightmare.

Jake pulled back farther, sensing the runabout directly behind him. The soldiers were still closing in, but they did not seem intent on stopping their retreat.

Jake took one more step back and reached out behind him. The hatch was closed. He turned, certain he hadn't left it that way. But it *was* closed, and there wasn't time to reach the controls, let alone do anything else. The approaching soldiers were only a few meters away now, with nothing to stop them from opening fire if he or Elliena made a wrong move.

"I wish Jedri were here," Elliena said, clasping Jake's arm as their backs touched the runabout's smooth, curved hull.

Jake blinked. "Who?"

"My uncle. He fought in the resistance, like Major Kira. My parents tell many stories about him, even when he's present. No, *especially* when he's around. They embarrass him all the time, but he truly *is* a great hero."

The soldiers halted their advance just a few meters away.

"What do you want with us?" Jake called out to them, sensing it was past time to do at least that much.

They seemed to look at one another for a moment, but not one of them said a word. That was when Jake began to notice certain peculiarities about them, like the fact that they looked almost identical to one another. He tried again, asking the same question, but as before, the Cardassians acted as if they hadn't understood a word.

Then a movement caught Jake's eye, a dark shape drifting in the mists, emerging on their right, showing a flash of color. He tugged at Elliena's arm and pointed. They watched carefully as the lone figure broke through the mist just behind the soldiers' left flank.

Jake didn't recognize the man, but he was clearly Bajoran, perhaps thirty-five and dressed in civilian clothing, and he was carrying an energy rifle.

"Jedri!" Elliena called out in relief. "Help us!"

"But . . . how?" Jake wondered out loud.

The Cardassians had turned toward the newcomer, but none of them took any action. For that matter, neither did Elliena's uncle Jedri.

More movement on Jake's right drew his attention. He strained his eyes to see, remaining as patient as he could while he waited for the new figure to get close enough, the mists to get thin enough. He realized he was watching a young Bajoran woman who was pointing her weapon at the soldiers—a woman who looked almost exactly like Major Kira, though she wore tattered civilian clothing and her dark hair was longer. But that, Jake knew, was impossible. At least it should have been. The two Bajorans seemed to have the Cardassians in a classic cross-fire pattern, but the odds were still clearly in the soldiers' favor.

"How did you get here?" Elliena called out to the man she thought to be her uncle.

No one answered. In fact, no one said or did anything. They all just stood there, as if they were waiting for instructions.

"Put down your weapons or they'll shoot!" Jake shouted at the Cardassian soldiers, thinking the threat might be worth a try.

Without hesitation, and much to Jake's surprise, the Cardassians did just that.

"Thank the Prophets!" Elliena said. "I can't believe it."

Jake couldn't either. He moved forward slowly, cautiously, then bent low to pick up one of the discarded weapons. The rifle was solid enough, but he couldn't find the firing mechanism, and the charge-level indicator was completely blank. Nevertheless, he pointed the weapon at the soldiers as he retreated back to Elliena's side.

"Major, what do we do now?" Elliena called.

Kira said nothing at all. In fact, she didn't move.

"They aren't real," Jake whispered to Elliena.

"Uncle Jedri?" Elliena called out, apparently unwilling to believe what Jake had said. Her call went unanswered.

"They look like cattle," Jake said, considering all seven visitors more closely.

"Like what?"

"Cows. Domesticated animals from Earth. They're sort of dumb and lethargic."

"Cows," Elliena repeated, trying out the word

while still staring at the Cardassians. "What do you do to get rid of—of five cows?"

"I'm not certain, but . . ." He stepped forward and yelled, "Shoo!" waving both hands at the soldiers. "Shoo! Scat! Get out of here! Go on, go!"

Elliena followed his lead. "Get going!" she called out, waving her arms. "Go away, far away!"

Remarkably, all five soldiers began to back away. Major Kira and Uncle Jedri simply stood there looking at each other as the Cardassians moved back and gradually vanished into the mist. Uncle Jedri finally turned and pointed his weapon at Elliena. Kira did likewise, but instead of firing they too began backing away, one step at a time, until they had vanished like the others.

Jake found himself trailing after the vanished figures. Elliena came with him, as if drawn toward the mystery. They continued for several paces, but stopped when it was clear there was nothing to see.

"I don't know what they were, but that wasn't my uncle," Elliena said. "He's never been indecisive."

"That woman didn't act like Major Kira, either. She didn't even look like Kira, exactly. I don't mean the obvious age difference. I mean her eyes, her expression—they just weren't right."

Elliena nodded, still staring into the clouds of mist that drifted before her. Jake took her hand and held it. Nothing in his experience had prepared him for the strange events taking place here, but he felt compelled to keep that fact a secret.

"I think we have to be careful of what we say," he

suggested. "Weren't we talking about Kira and your uncle just before they showed up?"

"Yes, we were." Elliena seemed to reflect on the matter, then said, "I guess we're lucky we weren't talking about the Jem'Had—"

"Don't say it!" Jake snapped, putting his hand gently over her mouth. "Don't even *think* about it. We weren't talking about Cardassians when the soldiers showed up. Someone might be monitoring our thoughts."

Elliena nodded, and he let go.

"You're right," she said. "Maybe we should talk about finding a way out of here instead."

"If my father were here, he'd know what to do," Jake said without thinking. Then he flinched as he realized what he'd done. He saw Elliena flinch at the same time. They waited for some imprecise facsimile of Captain Sisko to appear, but none did.

"I guess he's not going to show," Elliena said.

"Guess not."

"Jake, look there." Elliena tugged at Jake's hand. He lifted his eyes and saw two more figures approaching, coming out of the mists. They seemed particularly blurry and obscure, lacking detailed features of any kind, at least from what he could see of them so far. They vanished again as a fresh cloud of dense mist wafted over them. Then they reemerged, clearer now. Closer. Neither of them was his father, Jake was sure of that. There wasn't nearly enough bulk or height. He noticed that the figures weren't exactly walking, either, but instead seemed to be floating slowly along just above the surface, straight toward him. "Now what?" Jake grumbled.

"I don't know, but I've had more than enough excitement already," Elliena said.

"Me too. I say we get back inside the runabout until we can figure out what's going on."

"Sounds good to me."

Jake turned around—and froze. The *Rio Grande* had disappeared.

CHAPTER
20

"Go to impulse. Full sensor sweep," Commander Worf ordered as the *Defiant* burst from the mouth of the wormhole into the Gamma Quadrant.

"I'm not picking anything up in the immediate area," Kira replied after only a moment. "Going to long-range scan."

Worf leaned to one side of the *Defiant*'s command chair, his eyes moving from the view on the main screen to Dax's helm station directly ahead of him, then to the elbow-level instrument panels at his sides. He hadn't been off the *Enterprise* that long, but at times it seemed like ages. It felt good to be back aboard a starship, though in this case the reason was a particularly urgent one. He shifted his weight, feeling restless. Something inside him—a combination of Klingon blood and Starfleet training, perhaps, or the pulse of the engines in the deck beneath his feet—drove him to want to take action. He wasn't sure why, but he had always felt that way.

"Lieutenant Dax," he said, "do you have an approximate position for the planetoid you told the captain about?"

"I've already entered the heading."

Worf nodded, not the least bit surprised. "Major?" he asked.

"Still nothing out there," Kira replied.

"Very well. Engage at warp nine. Prepare for possible cloaking."

"Aye, sir," Dax acknowledged. The *Defiant* came about as the warp engines engaged, and the stars blurred into motion on the external viewscreen.

The journey would take hours, time enough to consider what might lie ahead. Somewhere out there were two Federation runabouts, a deadly phantom Klingon freighter, and two Klingon warships, all of which had apparently vanished from the immediate vicinity of the wormhole after arriving here. At least some of them had no doubt left of their own accord, but surely not all. And there might be other players as well. Renegade Rylep or Aulep ships, even Dominion vessels. Regardless, Worf had no intention of allowing an unwelcome fate to befall the Defiant.

"You have the conn, Major," he said, rising. Time to take a quick inspection tour of the ship. He headed for Engineering. The *Defiant* wasn't his, he knew, but for now it was his responsibility.

* * *

"Commander," Major Kira's voice said, following a chime from Worf's comm badge. Only an hour had passed since he left the bridge.

"What is it?"

"You might want to get back up here. I'm picking up a ship traveling at high warp, coming straight at us."

Worf nodded, mostly to himself. "I will be right there."

He arrived on the bridge seconds later. Kira looked over her shoulder, acknowledging him. "I'm getting a second ship directly behind the first one, but it's very faint, possibly a sensor echo. The first ship is big, possibly that Klingon attack cruiser. We'll know in a moment."

"Red alert," Worf ordered, on shipwide intercom. "All hands stand by."

A minute later Kira turned toward him once more. "It's Drokas's ship all right, but I still can't get an ID on the second contact—if it's there at all."

"What about visual?" Worf asked.

"Not yet."

"I would not be surprised if those ships are identical," Worf said, drawing the conclusion all too readily.

"Neither would I," Kira said. "What's that?" she added, observing something that made her sit up.

Worf let several seconds tick by. "Report!"

"Confirmed—warp torpedoes being fired by the lead ship," Kira said crisply. "They're firing at the second ship. Return fire verified." She paused for just an instant. "I'm reading at least one hit on the leader. It's dropping out of warp."

"And the second ship?"

"I'm still having trouble discerning it. It reads like a shadow of the first one. Both ships are dropping below light-speed."

"Estimated time to their position?"

"Two minutes, fourteen seconds," Dax replied.

"Adjust course to intercept. Shields at maximum."

Dr. Bashir entered the bridge and took a position close behind Worf's left shoulder. "Find something, Mr. Worf?"

"Yes," Worf said. "We are trying to ascertain what it is."

"Do you want to engage the cloak?" Odo asked, from his station at the Ops console.

A stealthy approach would help to keep them out of harm's way, but Worf wanted those ships to know that the *Defiant* had arrived on the scene. He had questions that needed answers, and he had to assume time was short. Besides, he'd had his fill of ghosts for a while.

"Negative," he said. "Bring us out of warp just outside of their weapon range."

Seconds later the *Defiant* slowed to impulse speed, and the stars became real again. "Arm all weapons," Worf said, wasting no time.

"That may provoke them," Dax cautioned, even as Odo went about the task.

"Perhaps," Worf said slowly. "But if it *is* Drokas,

he has already been in this area for some time. He may know where our runabouts are. If he is destroyed, he will not tell us anything."

"He might consider us an annoyance, or a threat, and try to destroy us," Odo said, as if to no one.

"Either way, I do not intend to let him prevent us from finding the captain and the others. If they want a fight," he said flatly, "I intend to give them one. If they require assistance, we will supply that as well."

"I have a visual on the second ship now," Kira reported, automatically putting the image on the screen. She had increased the viewer's magnification to reveal a second Klingon Vor'cha-class battle cruiser slowly emerging from behind the first like a moon orbiting a planet.

"I see," Worf said concisely, but he didn't like what he saw—two virtually identical Klingon vessels chasing each other, firing at one another. He already knew how that scenario could play out.

"Major, adjust sensors to scan for any additional energy anomalies out there. Odo, open hailing frequencies."

Both officers nodded and went to work. "Scanning," Kira said.

"No response to our hails," Odo said.

Worf watched the screen. There were any number of reasons why Drokas might not respond, and Worf didn't like any of them. "Major?"

"Nothing."

"I want full damage reports on each of those ships," Worf returned.

"Drokas's ship has already taken a beating," Kira reported. "I'm reading shields nearly depleted. Their warp core is intact, but their main engines are off-line. I'm also picking up numerous other systems failures, including aft disrupters. The second ship doesn't read, except as a very faint energy pattern. I can't see any damage at all."

"Just like the second Klingon freighter at the station," Worf said. "Can we acquire both targets?"

"Negative," Kira replied. "I can get a lock on Drokas's ship, but we'd be taking a primarily visual sighting on the other cruiser."

"I'm not sure it would do any good even if we could hit that second ship," Dax said. "Drokas's weapons don't seem to be having any effect on it."

"And direct hits on the attacking ship didn't do the *Toknor* any good back at the station," Odo said. "You can't shoot what isn't there."

"Commander, I'm picking up a fresh contact," Kira said abruptly. "Another energy reading, extremely faint."

"I'll try to get it on long-range visual," Dax offered, tapping at her controls. On the viewscreen a ship appeared, small but growing, and already recognizable: a Federation runabout.

"That looks like the *Rubicon,*" Bashir said, one hand gripping the back of Worf's command chair. He had been quietly observing, typically leaving tactical discussions to those who knew them best, but the excitement in his voice was clear and understandable, Worf thought. O'Brien and Bashir had become good friends in recent months. Up until this moment, no one had had any idea whether O'Brien and the captain were still alive. Worf saw the hope in the doctor's eyes, but he couldn't help thinking that perhaps it was a bit premature.

"If that's the *Rubicon,* we should have solid readings," Dax remarked, cooling everyone's enthusiasm.

"Agreed," Worf said. "Therefore we must assume that this is not truly one of our runabouts, that Drokas has some knowledge of this look-alike, and that he may have knowledge of the real *Rubicon,* since the one we're tracking seems to be following him."

"Or looking for us," Dax politely mentioned.

But as the runabout neared the cruiser's coordinates, it took up a position several thousand meters to starboard of the battle cruiser. Worf could see all three ships plainly on the viewscreen now.

"Still no answer to our hails from either of the Klingon cruisers or from that runabout," Dax said.

"Wait a minute," Kira said, concentrating on her screens as she tapped at the pads arrayed before her. "Drokas is up to something. I'm reading a massive energy buildup in the cruiser's warp core."

"I'm reading it too," Dax said. She turned and looked over her shoulder at Worf. "At this rate, it'll consume the containment fields and generators in a matter of minutes."

"Drokas's cruiser has engaged impulse engines," Kira said. "They're coming about. . . . Now they're moving toward the second cruiser."

"You don't suppose they're going to fly into that second cruiser and then blow themselves up?" Odo wondered aloud.

"That is a possibility," Worf said.

Dax shook her head. "No, I don't think that's it, but they may be doing something almost as crazy. It looks as if they're correcting their course to take them within a few hundred meters of the other cruiser—a near miss."

"I don't see what good that will do them," Odo said. "They don't have any weapons, they're badly damaged, and they've already—"

"They've jettisoned their warp core!" Kira said, cutting Odo off.

"It's headed straight for the second cruiser," Dax said. "I estimate sixty-four seconds to breach, sixty-three to impact."

"Drokas is using the most destructive weapon he has left against his opponent," Worf said, feeling a tinge of admiration.

"But they're sacrificing their only means of returning home," Bashir said, clearly grappling with the thought.

"Yes," Worf replied. "But if the plan is successful, they will have won."

"Not unless they can get a little more power out of their impulse engines," Kira said. "At this rate, they're going to get caught in their own blast."

"I'm sure that wasn't part of their plan," Bashir said, primarily to Worf.

Worf leaned forward, tightening one fist where it rested on the arm of the command chair. "Drokas!" Worf shouted at the screen.

"The channel is still open. He just isn't responding," Odo said.

"Drokas, listen to me! You are not thinking your actions through. Consider the mistakes of Dolras and the *Toknor,* and do not repeat them. We have to join forces. It is our only chance of defeating this adversary."

"It is a little late to join forces," Drokas said, finally facing Worf on the viewscreen. He looked a mess. Smoke and sparks filled the air on his bridge, and one crewman, visible at his post, had a bleeding wound on his left shoulder, where part of a bulkhead or ceiling panel had apparently fallen on him. Drokas himself wore a dark smudge on one side of his face, and his hair was wet and matted just behind his right ear.

"It is not too late," Worf said. "Allow us to help you. Trust me, Drokas."

"The cruiser is losing speed," Dax reported. "The warp core will go critical in forty-four seconds."

"How do I know I can trust you?" Drokas asked.

"You have already made that decision," Worf said.

Drokas frowned, then nodded once. "Very well."

Worf turned to his crew. "I do not want to drop our shields to beam all of them off the cruiser.

Lieutenant, go to full impulse, direct intercept course. Major, lock on to Drokas's cruiser with our tractor beam and try to extend our shields around them."

Instantly the *Defiant* leaped ahead, crossing the distance to the Klingon cruiser, vectoring just to the big vessel's starboard side. Worf watched the thin modulating light of the tractor beam touch Drokas's ship, then lost sight of it on the screen as the *Defiant* surged past the cruiser.

"We have them in tow," Kira said. "Shields extended, but their weight is straining our generators. We might all be in trouble when that core goes up."

"Four seconds," Dax counted.

Worf tapped at his own controls, and the screen displayed an aft view. Most of Drokas's ship was visible off the port side of the *Defiant*'s stern. Beyond it, the second cruiser floated in silence, as if patiently awaiting its fate. He couldn't see the jettisoned warp core anymore. It had already reached its target. Then the screen went blindingly bright as the intensity of the antimatter explosion lit the night.

"All hands, brace for impact!" Worf commanded, as the bridge crew grabbed anything stable. The shock wave arrived seconds later, a massive impact that seemed to slam into every part of the ship's armored hull at once. The bridge was cast in momentary darkness as the *Defiant* tried to shake itself apart. Then it was over; the lights came back on. The wave had passed.

Worf loosened his fierce grip on the arms of the

command chair and looked about. Major Kira had ended up on the floor, but she was getting up already, going back to her post.

Worf frowned. "Damage report."

"A few system overloads," Odo said. "Power grids, plasma conduits. Backups functioning properly. Injuries are minor."

Worf nodded in satisfaction. "What about Drokas?"

"The cruiser was torn loose from our tractor beam," Dax said. "It's drifting."

"The crew is all right, as far as I can tell," Kira said, still breathing hard. "I've terminated the tractor beam, and I'm reconfiguring our shields."

"Acknowledged," Worf said.

"How did you know Drokas would trust you?" Odo asked the commander, when a moment of silence had passed.

"Drokas has a great deal of experience. A warrior does not last that long without learning to judge those he encounters quickly and correctly."

"Commander, you aren't going to believe this, but that second cruiser is still there," Dax said, putting the image on the screen. Worf could see the phantom attack cruiser and the phantom *Rubicon* clearly. As far as he could tell, neither ship had changed a bit.

"Drokas has impulse engines online again," Kira reported. "He's coming about, but he's turning away from the other ships . . . and us."

"Hail him again," Worf said, letting irritation show in his tone, feeling better for it. Odo sent the message, and Drokas appeared on the screen once more.

"This is Commander Worf. We are willing to offer assistance. In return, we would like any information you have regarding our runabouts."

"Isn't that one of them?" Drokas asked.

"No," Worf said. "That is an energy echo of some kind, a ghost ship. We are interested in finding the real runabout. What do you know?"

Drokas narrowed his eyes. "It would appear you know more than we do." He sounded utterly cheerless. "Perhaps it is you who should explain all this to me."

Odo looked up. "We asked you first."

"We must know what has happened to Captain Sisko and the others," Worf said. "Until you have answers *for* us, do not require any *of* us."

"Then we have very little to talk about."

"Perhaps you are right," Worf said slowly.

"I'll say this for you, Worf: you are not what I would have expected."

"And you are everything I expected."

Drokas stared from the screen for a moment, silent, then nodded once, a barely perceptible movement, and signed off.

"Do you think he'll attempt another attack on the phantom?" Bashir asked.

Worf stared straight ahead. "No. Drokas no longer has the resources. And I believe he now knows that, even fully armed, attacking these phantom ships is suicide."

"So was attacking the station," Odo pointed out, "but that didn't stop Gowron and half the Klingon Empire from trying it a few months ago."

"Drokas is veering off," Kira said. "I think he's heading back toward the wormhole."

"The journey will take months at partial impulse," Dax said.

"Drokas is still being followed closely by the phantom warship," Kira added. "It's matching his speed and course."

"Any sign of hostility?" Worf asked.

"Not at the moment," Kira said, "but we've got movement out there. The phantom *Rubicon* is closing on our position."

"I don't think we should provoke them," Bashir suggested.

"Are we going after Drokas?" Kira asked, turning, looking at Worf with steady and impartial eyes. Clearly she had her own ideas as to what his answer should be, but Worf understood she would accept whatever command he gave.

"No," he said. That seemed to be the answer she hoped for. "We'll continue on course toward the planetoid."

"What about our friend out there?" Odo asked, nodding toward the screen. The ghostly image of the *Rubicon* floated there—real, but not real.

"Ignore the phantom, unless they give us reason to do otherwise," Worf replied. "Lieutenant Dax, you have your orders."

"Aye, sir," Dax responded.

The *Defiant* leaped to warp speed once more, then continued accelerating until it had achieved a factor of eight, more than one thousand times the speed of light. The phantom *Rubicon* followed along, maintaining the same speed and distance for the next several hours. It was still there when Worf gave the order to drop back out of warp.

"We're approaching the planetoid," Dax said a few moments later.

"One-quarter impulse power," Worf said. "Proceed to a standard orbit and begin scanning."

As the *Defiant* settled into orbit, Worf rose from the command chair and went to hover over Major Kira's shoulder. He watched the sensor displays for a time, looking in particular for the spectral signature of a federation hull.

"Anything at all?" he asked, after the first full pass.

"Scans are inconclusive," Kira said, "and I see no sign of our people, but something is definitely going on down there on that planetoid."

"Explain."

"Dozens of high-energy impulses are going off all over the place. Some of them are pretty intense. They seem concentrated in one area near the equator, and I'm detecting a region of uncharacteristic M-class atmosphere at those same coordinates. It's like a giant bubble filled with air."

"But how is that possible?" Bashir asked. "There isn't any natural phenomenon that could account for it, is there?"

"None that I know of," Kira replied.

"It is possible, however, that the others are down there," Worf said, studying the readings himself.

"Possible," Dax agreed. "But why aren't we reading the runabouts?"

"With all that plasma activity, I'm surprised we're reading anything," Kira said.

"But we can't very well continue on our way until we're sure about what's there," Bashir said, coming up behind Kira's other shoulder. "Not if there's the slightest chance."

"He's right," Dax said.

"Agreed," Worf said, turning. The other officers had known Sisko, Jake, and O'Brien much longer than he had, but he understood how they felt. "We'll stay until we've investigated the area. What's the status on our runabout shadow?"

"It's gone," Dax reported. "When we made orbit, it disappeared. I'm not reading any trace of it now."

"Are our transporters operative?"

"We'll have to manually adjust the frequencies to compensate for all the interference down there, but that shouldn't be difficult," Dax replied. "We can run a test to be sure."

"Open hailing frequencies," Worf told Odo, going back to the commander chair, settling into it. "Maximum gain. We shall see if anyone answers."

CHAPTER
21

"THEY'RE US, THEY'RE our doubles, just like the runabout and the other ships," O'Brien said, still gaping at the two figures who stood before him, less than five meters away. This close it was clear that while these two visitors from the mist were similar to the originals, they were not precisely correct. The hair, the eyes, even the uniforms didn't look quite right.

"What are you reading now?"

O'Brien groaned—caught napping again. He jerked the tricorder up and blinked it into focus, then tapped at the controls. "There's still too much local interference, but I am picking up traces of energy readings that are probably coming from our look-alikes. Beyond that, these two phantoms don't read at all."

"I'm not surprised."

"So what do we do with them?"

O'Brien watched Sisko as he seemed to consider the matter. "Hello there!" the captain sang out in a pleasant voice. He got no response.

O'Brien shrugged. "They might be good-looking, but they're not very friendly, are they?"

"No."

"You know, they say if you travel far enough, you'll eventually run across yourself," O'Brien said.

"Well, I guess it's true." Sisko continued eyeing the others closely. "But they aren't exactly like us, are they? For one thing, we're talking and they're not."

"Maybe they're just . . . shy."

"Maybe," Sisko said, taking a step to his right, away from O'Brien, to get a look at their visitors from another angle. As O'Brien watched, he was struck by the mental image of flat two-dimensional figures—of walking around to one side of these twins and finding only a pair of thin, vertical lines. He imagined that all of the images might have been that way, the other Klingon freighter, the other *Rubicon*. The idea seemed entirely possible. He stepped to the left to get a better look.

"They're three-dimensional," he mumbled, feeling slightly disappointed.

"Yes," Sisko said, as if he knew exactly what O'Brien meant. "But if you look closely you can almost see through them."

The doubles turned only their heads as they

watched the captain and the chief move about. O'Brien glanced back down at the tricorder, hoping for some unexpected breakthrough. His eyes went wide.

"Wait, I've got something," he said, still scanning. He turned the tricorder slightly to the right and adjusted the parameters.

"What now?"

"Nothing like these guys. I'm getting a bounce-back signal from about two thousand meters off. I can't get an exact fix."

"Scan for the *Rio Grande* at maximum range."

"Aye, sir," O'Brien said, complying. He found just what he was looking for. "There's something big out there, and from what I can tell it's about the same mass as the *Rio Grande*. But I'm not getting any power readings."

"Could be that damned interference again."

"Yes, sir, but an operational runabout should produce strong enough readings to get through all this."

"The ship might have been damaged getting here, just as we were. They may have crashed."

O'Brien saw nothing of the emotion he thought Sisko must be feeling behind those dark eyes. The chief only nodded, his own thoughts giving voice to what his captain wouldn't say. Then he thought to try his communicator. He tapped at the badge on his chest and called the runabout. No response.

"We'll have to give our two look-alikes another try," Sisko said. He stepped closer to his double and raised his voice. "Can you tell us why we're here? Are there any more beings like us here? Is there another ship like this one?"

Nothing.

"Just who are you people?" Sisko insisted, with audible annoyance this time. Again, nothing.

O'Brien had seen an expression similar to the look on the faces of these visitors somewhere before, but he hadn't been able to figure out where. Suddenly it occurred to him.

"Let me try something," he said, stepping forward. He pointed to himself with both hands. "O'Brien," he said. Then, "Sisko," he continued, pointing to the captain. He'd taught his daughter, Molly, the difference between Mommy and Daddy in much the same way, when her young eyes had looked at him the way these aliens did now. He pointed to them next. "And you are?"

He received no direct response, but the two lookalikes seemed to get excited. They exchanged glances, then pointed at each other. O'Brien repeated the entire exercise. This time the other "O'Brien" opened his mouth and, in a voice that sounded distant but otherwise much like the chief's own, said, "O'Brien."

"They're willing to learn, anyway," the chief said.

"I think you're on to something," Sisko said, letting a grin find his lips. He followed suit, stating his rank and name while pointing to himself, then putting the question to his double.

"Captain . . . Sisko," the other responded.

"It's like we're playing with babies," O'Brien said.

"Perhaps."

O'Brien brought his tricorder back up. He began tapping at it once more, readjusting the scanning parameters. "The electromagnetic impulses are going wild all over this area, more so than before." He held out the instrument and showed the reading to Sisko.

"You're saying there's a connection between those readings and our friends?"

"It's possible."

Sisko glanced up again. Then he touched O'Brien's arm. "Chief, look."

O'Brien followed the captain's gaze, found their look-alikes eagerly tapping at a newly materialized tricorder while eyeing the real Sisko and O'Brien repeatedly, as if making comparisons. Their expressions were more intense than O'Brien had expected.

"They don't look very happy," Sisko noted, clearly puzzled.

"Huh. I bet I don't either."

Then Sisko seemed to come to a conclusion. "I wonder," he said, rubbing his chin while his eyes moved from left to right. He lowered his hand, took a step forward, and grinned broadly. He kept grinning like a paid fool, and after only a few seconds the twins began to cheer up as well. Soon they were grinning in kind.

"Let's try something else," the captain said. He put one finger on the side of his nose, and the doubles carefully imitated the gesture. Next he put one hand on top of his head, the other on his belly, and began to rub. The twins did the same. "Curious," he said, tipping his head to one side.

"I'll say," O'Brien replied, giving up on the tricorder now. He put it away and looked back at the *Rubicon,* shaking his head, feeling a pang of frustration. He let his gaze wander up toward the hazy sky. None of this made sense. There was no question that they had been dealing with an intelligence that could control vast energies and reap great destruction, but that certainly didn't seem to be who they were facing right now. Which left some difficult unanswered questions lying about.

"Chief," Sisko said, breaking into O'Brien's thoughts, "why don't you try it."

It wasn't actually a question. "Whatever you say, sir, but if you ask me, this is no time for games." He thought for a moment, thought of Molly, then began vigorously rubbing his hands together. Both phantoms did the same.

"That's enough, Chief," Sisko said. A look of sudden revelation filled his features.

"What's going on?" O'Brien asked.

"Games!" Sisko said, grinning once more. "That's it!"

"Sir?" O'Brien asked again.

"Games. They're playing games. Learning the rules."

"They're willing to learn, but I'm not sure they're playing games."

Sisko faced their doubles again. He put one finger

in each of his ears, and his double did likewise. He pulled the fingers back out and laughed out loud, and his double laughed along with him—poorly at first, then better as Sisko swatted O'Brien on the back, his way of urging the chief to join in. O'Brien made a fair job of laughing, even though he still wasn't sure any of this was particularly funny. Their look-alikes were chuckling and slapping each other like old Academy chums.

They looked more like the real Sisko and O'Brien now, too, the chief noted. More human. They were better at this than Molly was when she was a baby, but it did seem to be how they learned. "I'm beginning to accept your theory, Captain," he said.

"Yes, that has to be it," Sisko nearly shouted. "They are trying to learn by doing, by observing, by playing and experimenting. Trial and error." He held his open hands out to the twins, gave them a nod, then waited. They stared at him for a long moment, then slowly looked at each other.

"Chief." He put his hands together. "Think of a game. Any game."

"Well, sir," O'Brien said, pondering the idea, "Molly likes to play catch. We sit on the floor and toss a big ball back and—"

"Wonderful!" Sisko burst out. "That's perfect!" He held both hands up like an old-fashioned traffic cop. "Everybody wait right here!" Then he turned toward the *Rubicon* and broke into a run.

CHAPTER

22

AT A FULL sprint Sisko quickly covered the distance back to the *Rubicon*. He rushed aboard and made his way straight to the replicator, where he set about adjusting the unit's program parameters. It took several moments, longer than he would have liked, but finally he gave it a try. What he got wasn't exactly what he'd hoped for, but on the second attempt he watched with delight as a genuine regulation baseball—white with red stitches—appeared in the replicator's open chamber.

He picked the ball up and held it in his palm, felt its familiar weight and mass, the slight elasticity of its surface when he gave it a hard squeeze. "Just about right," he muttered, smiling in satisfaction. Then he spun around and headed back out through the hatch.

"Chief," Sisko said as he arrived among the others once more. "We have to get everyone spread out, four ways. I'd say about half a dozen meters apart for starters. If we separate ourselves first, the our doubles might do the same."

"All right, Captain, whatever you say."

"It'll be fine, Chief. You'll see." Sisko was still smiling.

O'Brien walked backward several paces, then paused, and Sisko attempted to coax their doubles into doing the same. After a brief period of blinking puzzlement the look-alikes moved apart to complete the square.

"All right, Chief," Sisko said, "catch!" He tossed the baseball, underhand. O'Brien caught it easily enough.

"Now throw it back."

O'Brien did as ordered. Sisko caught the ball, turned toward his double, and tossed it underhand again. The other Sisko just stood there as the ball bounced off his chest, then rolled on the ground. Sisko did a bit more pointing and beckoning. Finally his double bent down, picked the ball up, and threw it back to Sisko. His toss went a bit wide, and the captain had to lunge to his left to make the catch, but essentially the experiment was proving itself a success. He threw again, back to O'Brien.

"Now throw it to your double, and we'll see if they, you know, catch on."

O'Brien rolled his eyes at the pun, but then he turned and gently threw another underhand pitch.

His own double nearly managed to catch the ball, dropping it only after it bounced out of his hands.

"It takes a little practice," O'Brien told his twin, who was looking at the two genuine Federation officers with an expression usually reserved for questioning the origin of the universe.

Sisko pointed, indicating that he wanted O'Brien's double to throw to O'Brien, and the ball changed hands. With the next pitch it came back to Sisko. He couldn't have been more thrilled. But before he could say any more, his comm badge chirped.

"Defiant to Captain Sisko," Commander Worf's voice said, clouded slightly by static but clear enough to read. It caught Sisko off guard, but he recovered instantly.

"Yes, Commander!" he replied, tapping his badge active. "Chief O'Brien and I were forced down onto the surface of the planetoid. The area we're in seems stable at the moment, and we're all right. But I didn't think we could get a comm signal ten feet in all this interference."

"Our signal was blocked until just a moment ago," Worf reported.

Sisko looked more closely at their doubles as the ball went around again, one easy, arching underhand throw, then another. This time the look-alikes both caught the ball, if somewhat awkwardly. They really *were* beginning to catch on, but that wasn't all. They looked very much like him and the chief now, so they seemed to be getting better at that, too.

"Captain, we encountered two Klingon Vor-cha-class attack cruisers, one commanded by Captain—"

"Drokas," Sisko said. "Yes, Mr. Worf, we've met, but to be honest, I didn't think he would last this long."

"Only Drokas's ship registered as normal on our sensors," Dax explained. "The other was a phantom, like the second Klingon freighter we saw at the station."

"Did you sustain any damage?"

"No," Worf said. "The cruisers fought each other. Ultimately Drokas retreated, but the second ship went after him."

"That makes sense," Sisko said.

"It does?" Dax asked.

"Absolutely."

Sisko's twin made a great catch using only one hand, and the captain let out a cheer.

"Captain," Worf said, sounding puzzled, "may I ask what are you doing?"

"We're having a game of catch, Commander."

"Catch?" Worf repeated.

Sisko allowed himself a chuckle. "Yes. I'll be glad to show you what it is—that is, as soon as we're done here. I've got some other students at the moment. And we still have a search to conduct."

"Yes, sir. We have already begun a full scan of your area."

As the ball flew again, Sisko looked at O'Brien.

"You know, Chief, these guys are pretty good at this."

"They're pretty good at playing guns, too," O'Brien reminded him. "Or their friends are." Sisko nodded. He caught the ball again, then swung low, past his knee, sending it sailing back to O'Brien once more.

"Mr. Worf," Sisko said into the comm badge, "whatever you do, don't fire at or attack anything—runabouts, Klingon cruisers, duplicate *Defiant*s—nothing. Especially if it doesn't read one hundred percent real on your sensors. The entities controlling the phantoms will think you're trying to teach them something or that you're playing a game with them, and they'll just join in. That's what happened to the Klingon freighter, to Drokas, and possibly to Jake and Elliena. I believe this planetoid is some kind of . . . of nursery . . . full of children, hundreds of them. Maybe thousands."

Sisko glanced at O'Brien and found a worried look on his face.

"What is it, Chief?"

"I was just thinking that I'd hate to meet their parents."

Sisko watched his twin catch the ball once more, then toss it to him—a nice, steady throw. Sisko caught it easily. "They learn by emulation," he went on. "They're very curious and . . . playful. I'm trying to get through to them. I'm hoping they can give us some information about the *Rio Grande*. It's got to be here somewhere. There's even a good chance that Jake and Elliena are unharmed, just as we are, provided they didn't do anything foolish."

"Since when do teenagers do anything foolish?" O'Brien said grimly.

"Captain, if what you say is true, it could account for some of the problems other races in neighboring sectors have been having lately," Major Kira interjected. "The Aulep and Rylep, for example, and the Beshiel."

"The three of them wouldn't stop arguing," Dax said.

"You wouldn't believe the trouble we had getting away from the station," Kira said. "And I haven't even told you about the Klingons and the Ferengi."

"Who are the Beshiel?" Sisko asked.

"I'll explain later," Kira said. "But the Beshiel, the Rylep, and the Aulep have been encountering look-alike ships and blaming each other, of course. They'll be interested to learn they were wrong, and I'll enjoy telling them."

"Oh?" Sisko said, intrigued. He caught the ball, turned, gently threw it.

"Captain," Dax broke in, "I'm reading two new life signs not far from your position. It might be Jake and Elliena, but I can't get a positive identification."

O'Brien was already opening his tricorder and beginning to scan. "That agrees with my readings," he said.

"Dax, the interference seems to oscillate," Sisko

said. "Or it's being controlled. I want you to do another scan. See if you can find a window big enough to get a positive lock so that we can use the transporter."

"If nothing changes I should be able to," Dax replied. "But it might take some time."

"Lieutenant, why don't we try using my tricorder along with the ship's sensors to triangulate?" O'Brien suggested.

"That should work," Dax said.

"Good," Sisko said, pleased that his nearly automatic faith in his people had once more proved well founded. "So what are you waiting for?"

Sisko held the ball while O'Brien tapped at his tricorder and moved it from left to right front of him. "Transmitting data now," the chief said.

"I think we've got them," Dax said.

"Can you get a good enough lock to attempt transport?" Sisko asked.

"I believe so," Dax replied.

"Then try to beam them directly here," Sisko said. "As soon as you're ready."

"I've got them, Benjamin," Dax said. "They should be showing up right about . . . now."

Jake and Elliena suddenly materialized directly between Sisko and O'Brien. The only problem lay in the direction they were facing.

"Dad! Chief!" Jake yelled, as he came to realize what had happened. He started forward—toward the look-alikes.

"No, Jake, wait!" Sisko called after him. "I'm here, behind you. Those two aren't real."

Jake spun around wide-eyed, as did Elliena. Then they both started toward the real Sisko, though at a slightly slower pace. Sisko put his arms out, and Jake moved solidly into his father's embrace. Then he freed up an arm and pulled Elliena into the huddle. The hug lasted for a very long moment.

"Sisko to *Defiant*. We have Jake and Elliena with us, and they appear to be in good shape. Nice work."

"Yes, sir," Worf said. "Do you wish us to assist with repairs to the *Rubicon,* or should we beam you aboard?"

"For the moment, neither," Sisko replied. "We have a little unfinished business here. Stand by."

"I know what you mean about the doubles," Jake said excitedly. "In fact, we've been gaining a lot of experience with them. You wouldn't believe . . ."

He fell silent as Elliena put her hand on his shoulder and pointed toward the mist behind them. Sisko turned to find yet another Jake and Elliena slowly appearing there, walking toward them into existence. They looked almost precisely like the originals.

"So I see," Sisko said.

"Dad, they're okay. In fact, they're fascinating!"

"They are," Elliena verified. "We've been talking to them, sort of. It's amazing how easily they can learn to communicate."

"We've been learning all sorts of things about them, and they've been learning from us."

"You've been communicating with them? How?" Sisko asked.

Elliena looked at Jake.

"Well," Jake said, "we've been using sign language, but they're speaking a few words, too. And we think they have some empathic ability. I'm sure they could learn just about any language. I wish I had their ability."

"We still don't know who or what they are," Sisko said.

"Ahh, that's not exactly true," Elliena said.

"What do you mean?" Sisko asked.

"Well, we've got a pretty good idea who they are," Jake said.

Chief O'Brien wandered closer, followed by his double and Sisko's. The captain realized the eight of them were beginning to form quite a crowd. "Explain," he said.

"We're still guessing at a lot of this," Jake said. "And I'm not sure we've got the parts we've got quite right, but—" He stopped himself, apparently aware that he was babbling. Sisko waited patiently. Jake started over. "Okay, this planetoid seems to be an extragalactic spaceship of some kind. Probably from M-31 in the Andromeda galaxy, as far as I've been able to calculate from its path and direction. But this ship isn't like anything we've seen before."

"You can say that again," O'Brien said. "And neither are they," he added, indicating their attentive doubles.

"This planetoid is a generational colony ship," Elliena said. "These beings are part of a very advanced, very long-lived race that was sent out across the void ages ago."

"We've had colony ships, and so have other races," O'Brien said.

"I know, but when this planetoid was launched, its passengers were still embryos," Jake said. "Every one of them. I don't think there were ever any adults aboard."

"Now those embryos are growing, developing into children," Elliena said. "Brilliant children, who are quite busy at present discovering themselves and this new galaxy."

"A little like teenagers, I guess," Sisko said with a smile.

"Well, sort of," Jake said. "We think they're nearly mature enough to begin looking for a suitable site for their colony, although to them, 'nearly' might mean a human century or two."

"The important thing is, they aren't here to hurt anyone. We just have to try to understand them and help them understand us," Elliena said.

"Then neither of you perceives these beings as a threat?" Sisko asked. Jake and Elliena both shook their heads.

"Watch this," Jake said. He winked at his father and the chief, then turned to Elliena, gently put his arms around her, and kissed her. They held the kiss for several seconds, but even before they parted, their doubles had begun to do the same thing. Sisko shook his head and frowned, but then he let a grin slip.

"I'll stick with playing catch," O'Brien said.

"Me too, Chief," Sisko said. Then he tapped at his comm badge once more. "Sisko to *Defiant*."

"Worf here, Captain. Is everything all right?"

"Yes, Commander. Quite all right, in fact."

"Are you ready to begin repairs to the *Rubicon*?"

"Of course. We'll start that task when you beam down," Sisko said. "Right now I've got to get Jake and Elliena organized." He turned to the two teenagers and showed them each a wry grin. "We have a new mission here, and I'm assigning them to it, along with some of the rest of us, of course. They seem to be the experts. We have a lot of orientation work to do."

"Acknowledged," Worf said.

"Interesting," Sisko heard Dax say.

"We're staying here?" O'Brien asked, apparently somewhat chagrined. "For how long?"

"I think we can all stick around for a little while, Chief. This takes priority."

"Yes, sir," O'Brien said. "But what exactly are we going to do?"

"We have a chance to make some very important friends here. A chance to make sure the first extragalactic settlers to this galaxy get off on the right foot. Not to mention making life easier for some of the local inhabitants along their path. And besides, you're never too old, or too young, to learn something new. I'm sure we can all learn a lot from one another."

O'Brien nodded. "I've seen what they can do with a little energy. And with the Dominion barking at our heels, friends like these could really come in handy."

"My thoughts exactly," Sisko said.

"Stand by to receive away team," Worf informed them.

"We're on our way," Kira said. "Is there anything you need?"

"No. Major, wait!" Sisko said, considering Jake and Elliena once more. "I do have an extra little job for you before you transport."

"Go ahead," Kira answered.

Sisko smiled to himself. "I want you to see if the *Defiant*'s replicators can make . . . a bat."

"A bat, sir?"

"I believe a bat is a small, winged earth rodent," Worf said.

"No," Sisko said. "A baseball bat."

"Aye, sir," Kira replied. "I'll see what I can do. *Defiant* out."

Sisko looked to O'Brien. The chief winked at him, then turned and stepped back several paces. When he was in position, he turned around again, tossed the ball up in the air once, and caught it. Then he set his jaw a little to one side, bent slightly forward, and trained his eye on his double, who was already backing up, returning to his corner of their imaginary diamond.

"Captain," he said.

"Yes, Chief?"

"I think we're gonna need gloves, too."

Sisko broke into a chuckle.

O'Brien pulled back and let one fly, overhand.

Making up, pressing to the corner of their image,
her stature.

"CONSOL," he said.

"No. Children—"

"I think we're people read grown, now."

Babe broke and ... smoke

C threes pulled his hand before his own hand.

ALSO AVAILABLE!

STAR TREK®

#83

HEART OF THE SUN

by
Pamela Sargent and George Zebrowski

Available from
Pocket Books Star Trek

The following is a preview of
Heart of the Sun. . . .

Lieutenant Commander Scott was in engineering, having left Uhura in charge of the bridge. He had intended to run a few standard maintenance checks, having not had much opportunity to check the system over thoroughly while on the surface of Tyrtaeus II. Nothing very important in the checks he and his crew were running; they were the equivalent of polishing the surface of a beloved shuttlecraft, a routine task that had to be done from time to time, for the welfare of the caretaker's soul if nothing else.

Lieutenant Tristram Lund came and stood next to him; the blond man pressed his fingers to one panel. "Everything's working just fine," Lund said.

"Aye, laddie," Scotty said, having expected no less of his engines. "Might as well do some more sensor scans of that asteroid, then. The science officers can always use more data."

It had not escaped Scott from the start that the mobile possessed an advanced drive system that somehow did not reveal more than the impulse principle—not yet, anyway. He was curious to see if he could discover whether it had any interstellar capacity, or was merely a relativistic vessel.

Suddenly his instruments were showing him that the

mobile's drive system was capable of something more. Scotty peered at the readings, glanced at the nearest viewscreen, then gazed at his instruments again.

"Will you look at that," Lieutenant Lund muttered at Scotty's right, but the chief engineer had seen what the instruments were telling him even before he spoke. The mobile's drive system was suddenly casting a powerful field around the asteroid, a field more powerful than any use he could imagine for such a vehicle. As he started to scan the field's structure, it abruptly winked off.

"Well," Scotty said, "it doesn't need that much protection for space travel." He hit his console's communicator panel. "Engineering to bridge. Were you scanning that alien thing just now?"

"We saw it," Uhura's voice replied.

"Massoud here," Ali Massoud said. "That field might come up again. It might be a good idea to get that landing party out of there, and fast."

"Just what I was thinking," Scotty replied. "Uhura, open an emergency hailing frequency to the captain."

"Done, Mister Scott."

"Enterprise to Captain Kirk. Captain!"

"Kirk here." The captain's voice seemed faint.

"Scott here. I'd advise all of you to beam out right away. A strong field of some kind just went on and off around that alien thingee without any warning at all. It might trap you inside if it comes on again. Did you notice anything from in there?"

"Nothing," Kirk replied. "We can't accomplish anything more here, anyway. Preparing to beam aboard. Kirk out."

Scotty turned back to his instruments, watching to make sure that the team was beamed back safely. He held his breath, afraid that the field might wink on again. Something about the way it had come on and off had reminded him of automatic equipment being tested, as if the alien vessel was preparing for some important action.

"Survey team aboard," the voice of Kyle announced over the communicator, but Scotty already knew that from his instruments. He stared at the sensor readings, wondering what the alien might do now, but the field failed to come on again. He shook his head in puzzlement.

"Lund," he said to the lieutenant, "take charge here. I'm going up to the bridge."

Kirk was sitting at his station when Scott reached the bridge. Spock was with Ali Massoud and Myra Coles, reviewing the sensor scan records; Wellesley Warren and Cathe Tekakwitha stood with Uhura. Lieutenant Riley had remained on duty as navigator while Sulu and Rand were conferring with the captain.

"Captain," Scotty said as he came up to Kirk's station, "that thingee out there seems determined to head right into the sun. Did you find anything inside that might help prevent it?"

Kirk shook his head. "Nothing. We couldn't have stayed there much longer. It was too . . . disorienting."

"To put it mildly," Sulu added. "Amazing how much better we started to feel as soon as we were back aboard."

"Permission to speak, Captain," Myra Coles said. Scotty turned toward the woman, noting that she continued to adhere to Starfleet form of address, although she seemed to resent the formality. Bonny lass that she was, she could also be as prickly as a patch of briars. She was used to being a leader, he supposed, and it had to be hard for her to bow to someone else's authority.

"Permission granted," Kirk replied, sounding annoyed.

Coles said, "What especially worries me now is that if that field comes on again as strongly as we measured it, and the alien asteroid does strike the sun, the field-effect might either diminish or increase our star's output."

Scotty nodded grimly. "I've been thinking the same thing."

"It might not affect it for long," Coles went on, "but it could be long enough to face the people of my world with some very unpleasant climatic changes."

"What do you think of that, Mister Spock?" Kirk asked.

"I agree with Miss Coles. Indeed, I recommend that the object be diverted from its course right away, when it will not take much of an angle to divert it. Trying to do so even several hours from now will present many more difficulties."

"But we don't know what we're dealing with," Janice Rand objected.

"Quite right, Yeoman Rand," Spock said, "which makes it all the more imperative that we start doing what we can immediately, so that we can determine what we will be permitted to do."

"Permitted?" Myra Coles asked.

"Aye, permitted," Scotty responded. "Lassie, we're dealing with intelligence that won't show itself."

She gave him an annoyed look.

"And also with systems that appear savvy enough," Sulu added, "to deal with our efforts."

"Spock?" Kirk said.

"We will learn more by seeing what we can do," the Vulcan said. "And, given the possible effect that the alien worldlet might have on this system's star, we should act immediately."

Kirk stood up. "Well, then, let's take a direct approach, by strapping impulse boosters on the outside of the asteroid and changing its course."

"Aye," Scotty said. "Just what I was about to recommend."

"And once we've diverted it," Kirk continued, "we can spend more time investigating it."

"Let's consider what is going on here," Myra Coles said, moving away from Ali Massoud and closer to Wellesley Warren. "We were to investigate this object. Now we have to divert it from its course." She glanced at the other Tyrtaean for moral support. "Captain, is it possible that you might have caused this problem by disturbing this alien artifact?"

"Wait, now," Scotty cut in, "that's hardly fair, lassie. We all wanted to explore that thing." She gave him another hostile look.

"The unknown always has risks," Sulu said.

"And I must remind you," Kirk said, "that you and Aristocles Martine insisted that Tyrtaeans be part of this investigation, not to direct it."

Coles's gray eyes flashed. "Yes, Captain. But I also advised against going inside the worldlet. How do you know that your entering it didn't somehow cause that field to come on? Your actions might be partly responsible for the danger of the field-effect to our sun."

"Myra," Warren said in a low voice, "accusations aren't going to do us any good now. That field might have come on anyway." She shot an angry look at her aide. He continued, "If you'd seen how strange it was inside, how alien—" He paused. "I wonder if anything we've done has affected it, if we can actually affect it at all."

Kirk held up a hand. "I have ordered that we divert the object, Miss Coles. Do you have an alternative course of action to recommend?"

She was silent for a few moments. Scotty felt the tension on the bridge. The captain was keeping himself admirably calm, all things considered, but he would expect no less of Jim Kirk.

"Perhaps," Myra Coles said at last, "we should all just go away and leave this thing alone."

"In the hope that it will stop whatever it's doing?" Kirk's voice was sharper this time. "That would hardly seem the wisest course of action," Spock added gently.

"If it does stop then, if it does change course, it'll prove I was right. If there's intelligence there, it won't go into the sun. It will save itself."

Kirk said, "And if it doesn't, we'll lose all chance of investigating it further, as well as risking its field coming on again and possibly affecting your sun." He drew his brows together. "You've offered your opinion, Miss Coles. I choose to reject your advice. I am now going to plan the details of how to divert the worldlet with Lieutenant Commander Scott and Commander Spock. Remain here with Mister Massoud if you like, doing what you can to assist him, or go to your quarters if you prefer—but do not interfere with my orders, or I will be forced to confine you to quarters and then return you to your planet—and that will delay us even more. And time is growing short."

Myra Coles's face paled. Scotty expected her to storm off the bridge. He almost hoped that she would; then the captain could proceed without any more of her meddling.

"Captain," Warren said then, "we've all been under pressure. I think we all have legitimate fears about the asteroid, whether we're willing to admit to them or not."

Kirk gazed directly at Coles. "I meant what I said," he murmured. "You agreed to accept my authority when you came aboard. Either make yourself useful here or return to your quarters."

She lowered her eyes, having the grace to look chagrined. "I'll remain on the bridge for now," she murmured. "I'm sorry, Captain. I won't interfere."

Kirk said, "Now let's get down to deciding exactly how to keep that thing from immolating itself."

That was more like it, Scotty thought with relief.

Look for STAR TREK Fiction from Pocket Books

Star Trek®: The Original Series

Star Trek: The Next Generation®

Star Trek®: Voyager™

Flashback • Diane Carey
The Black Shore • Greg Cox
Mosaic • Jeri Taylor

#1 *Caretaker* • L. A. Graf
#2 *The Escape* • Dean W. Smith & Kristine K. Rusch
#3 *Ragnarok* • Nathan Archer
#4 *Violations* • Susan Wright
#5 *Incident at Arbuk* • John Greggory Betancourt
#6 *The Murdered Sun* • Christie Golden
#7 *Ghost of a Chance* • Mark A. Garland & Charles G. McGraw
#8 *Cybersong* • S. N. Lewitt
#9 *Invasion #4: The Final Fury* • Dafydd ab Hugh
#10 *Bless the Beasts* • Karen Haber
#11 *The Garden* • Melissa Scott
#12 *Chrysalis* • David Niall Wilson

Star Trek®: New Frontier

#1 *House of Cards* • Peter David
#2 *Into the Void* • Peter David
#3 *The Two-Front War* • Peter David
#4 *End Game* • Peter David

Star Trek®: Day of Honor

Book 1 *Ancient Blood* • Diane Carey
Book 2 *Armageddon Sky* • L. A. Graf
Book 3 *Her Klingon Soul* • Michael Jan Friedman
Book 4 *Treaty's Law* • Dean W. Smith & Kristine K. Rusch